Michal, Princess

Marilyn Kay Stout

Decatur, Michigan

For information write:

JENNKAY Publishers
19995 Marcellus Hwy.
Decatur, Michigan 49045

Library of Congress Catalog Card Number:97-73559

ISBN: 1-891049-01-1

Printed in the United States of America

Books available from JENNKAY Publishers:

Asenath, Daughter of Egypt is the story of the daughter of Egypt's high priest of the sun god Ra. Asenath is wed to Joseph, one of Jacob's twelve sons, a believer in Jehovah, the true and living God. It portrays her struggle between her idolatry and her husband's faith in Jehovah God. $8.95

Michal, Princess is the story of the younger daughter of Saul, Israel's first king, and first wife of David, Israel's best known king. It tells the tale of the tragedies and triumphs of her life as she grows in faith in God. $8.95

The Cord of Scarlet is the story of Rahab's faith from the fall of Jericho until her death. It presents the conflict between her past life as a pagan harlot of the Canaanites and her new life of faith in the God of the Hebrews. $8.95

Coming in 1998:

Dear Jennifer is the true story of Jennifer Kay Stout's life, compiled mostly from her own journals and diaries. It is an excellent book for parents and young people alike illustrating the questions and battles of a young girl's life and the answers she finds in Jesus Christ and God's Word. This book fulfills Jennifer's prayer as expressed in her Bible study journal the day before the Lord took her to heaven in a tragic automobile accident: **"God, will you allow me to have a part in giving the gospel to those who have never heard?"**

To order send check or money order to:

JENNKAY Publishers
19995 Marcellus Hwy.
Decatur, Michigan 49045

Please enclose $3.00 shipping for orders up to three books.

MICHAL, PRINCESS

PART ONE

"My voice shalt thou hear in the morning, O LORD; in the morning will I direct my prayer unto thee, and will look up."
Psalm 5:3

CHAPTER 1

THE PRINCESS

"The king's daughter is all glorious within: her clothing is of wrought gold." Psalm 45:13

Shadows slanted across the palace courtyard drawing stripes of sunlight and shade along the smooth stones. The younger daughter of Saul, King of Israel, ran along a stripe of sunshine, then veered toward a large doorway, where the heavy wooden door stood ajar. She slipped into the cool corridor, and her small, silk slippered feet padded quickly toward a strip of light showing beneath another large, wooden door. A small hand reached for the latch, and with a great push she moved the door and released a flood of light into the gloom of the corridor.

The room before the princess was long and low ceilinged with a narrow wooden table running the length of it. Two servants who stood in attendance at the table scowled at her as she ran past them. The children of the king had been fed in their own dining room an hour before. The grown sons of the king and their wives now supped with their father and mother.

The princess threw herself against her mother's reclining form and buried her face in the rich folds of her mother's gown. Silent sobs shook her small shoulders. Gently Ahinoam, the queen, pulled the small princess upright and brushed the straying hair back from her wet face. After a pause the adult conversation resumed, and the queen asked gently, "Why do you weep?"

"He hit me with a stick, Mother!" the princess sniffed.

The queen glanced toward the others engaged in conversation at the table and rose to her feet. "Come," she told the princess, and led her from the room, down the dark corridor, and through another doorway. This room was smaller than the dining room. A large, down-covered bed stood along one wall.

The stone walls were plastered and hung with rich tapestries. The queen sat upon a pile of cushions and motioned for the princess to sit at her side. She looked toward the tall black eunuch at the door and motioned him to leave.

Again the mother asked quietly, "Why do you weep?"

"Eshbaal hit me with a stick," the child answered.

"Who are you, child?" the queen asked.

The little princess blinked and creased her forehead. "I am Michal, Mother."

"And who are you, Michal?" the queen repeated.

Michal sat quietly for a moment, deep in thought. She looked at her mother with her forehead still creased and answered, "I am a princess, daughter of Saul the King of Israel." She squinted and bit her lip as she waited to see if this answer was satisfactory.

"How old are you, Michal, princess?" the queen asked.

"I have had six years, Mother."

The queen looked gravely into her daughter's eyes. "Then you are full old enough to behave properly."

"But it was Eshbaal who hit..." the child began.

"Cease!" said the queen. Michal closed her mouth and lowered her eyes.

"A daughter of King Saul does not weep before the servants," the queen said.

"But it hurt, Mother," Michal protested mildly.

"Yes, child," the queen said gently, lifting Michal's chin to bring her eye to eye. "But a princess must not show her pain. A princess must bear the hurt inside and let nothing show before the servants, the subjects, those of common rank." The queen closed her eyes for a moment. "When it hurts, Michal, lift your chin and try hard not to let it show. And the more it hurts, the higher you must lift your chin. Do you understand?"

"Yes, Mother," the small princess answered as her heart cried in confusion.

"Good. Let us see how well you understand." The queen

stood and called the tall black slave into the room.

"Fetch a whip, Zerah," she commanded.

Michal stood quietly, waiting in dread. Zerah reentered bearing a long, thin leather strap and stood at attention before the queen.

"Whip the legs of the princess," the queen told him, gesturing toward Michal. Then she smiled wanly at the princess and said, "Lift your dress, child."

Michal obeyed, clutching the hem of her dress to her chest and closing her eyes. Zerah hesitated a moment and then the lash stung the back of Michal's legs. The tears sprang instantly to her eyes, but she sniffed and swallowed and lifted her chin.

"Again," said the queen.

Once again the whip was laid against Michal's legs. She clenched her teeth together hard and lifted her chin higher.

"Again," the queen said.

Michal wondered if she could live if struck again, but the lash was delivered and she found that her chin would lift yet higher. The tears found their way through her tightly squeezed eyelids, but no sound escaped her throat. She would please her mother. She would not show her pain before a servant.

"Enough," said the queen, and the tall black man bowed and stepped back. She waved him from the room and took her small daughter into her arms.

"Now you may cry, Michal," the queen said kindly.

"I do not need to cry, now, Mother," the child answered bravely.

"That is well," her mother answered. "But there may be times that you will need to cry. Here," she motioned about the room, "in privacy, without servants, it is well to cry."

The queen released her daughter and stepped away. "Go, now," she said. "Go to your rooms and sleep." She called Zerah and instructed him to accompany the princess.

Michal walked silently along the corridors and up the

4

wide staircase to the rooms of the king's daughters. She stood before the door, waiting for the slave to open it for her. With his large hand on the latch, Zerah looked sadly at her with moist black eyes.

"Forgive me, Princess," he said softly. He opened the door and Michal entered the room.

*** ***

A servant woman jerked the comb through Michal's thick brown hair. It hurt. But Michal sat still upon the stool as her hair was plaited and wrapped around her head, then covered with a scarlet veil. The comb was turned to the hair of the elder princess, Merab, as another servant slipped a garment of many colors over Michal's head.[1]

The day was one of joy in the palace of Gibeah. Jonathan, the eldest son of King Saul and heir to the throne of Israel, was to be wed. The two little girls would be present at the festivities of a wedding feast for the first time. Impatient with the primping of the servant women, Michal ran to the door where Zerah stood, arms doubled across his broad chest, eyes staring at some invisible point that he alone could see.

"Take me to the feast, now, Zerah," she said.

Zerah's black eyes smiled at her and his white teeth flashed in his ebony face. "Yes, princess," he answered. "I will take you as soon as these wise women deem you fit to appear at such a grand occasion."

Michal frowned. She returned to the women who fussed over her sister. "Come, Merab," she urged. "We will miss the feast." Merab turned her large blue eyes to Michal. Her fair hair was braided and piled high upon her brow. At nine years of age she looked a young woman already and displayed the grace of

---

[1] 2 Samuel 13:18

her station.

"We would not do honor to our dear Jonathan to appear at his wedding less than our best."

When all preparations had been completed Zerah led the two small princesses to the banqueting hall. They entered the large room through a series of columns. Gleaming brass lamps circled the room, aiding the daylight to brighten the room to a brilliance. Colorful hangings descended from the marble pillars. The chaises upon which the guests reclined were of gold and silver, cushioned with cunning embroidery. Michal was always awed to enter here and wonder at the whole reflected in the polished marble floor. It was as if another celebration took place beneath their feet, with the people hanging upside down.

The small princesses took their places with the king and queen. Spread before them were roasted meats, vegetables steamed to perfection, fresh fruits and vegetables, breads, raisins, figs, and pomegranates. Nectars filled the tall goblets of gold and silver. Michal lay quietly upon the small couch and watched herself in the golden goblet before her. A slight twist of her head would contort her reflection, bringing laughter in her belly, but never to her lips.

Jonathan's bride, Neziah, had been carefully chosen for her family and upbringing. Careful consideration must be taken for the qualities of a future queen. Neziah had both family and personal merit, as Jonathan had confided to his little sister. Her family was of Lodebar, and her father was Machir, the son of Ammiel.

"My father has chosen a bride both wisely and well," Jonathan had told Michal with a smile. "To marry whom one must, as well as whom one wishes is pleasant indeed."

Although the eldest of Saul's sons, Jonathan was the third to wed. Malchishua and Abinadab had both taken wives and fathered sons. Jonathan and his firstborn son, however, would inherit the throne of Israel.

Neziah and her family sat at the table adjoining that of the king's family. All guests were present. Quiet conversation bode the wait for the entrance of the bridegroom.

A burst of trumpets drew all eyes to the large bronze doors which swung slowly open as Jonathan and his companions entered the hall. Exclamations reverberated throughout the room at Jonathan's wedding garments and chains of gold. His companions waited as he approached the table of Neziah. Extending his right hand, decked with jeweled rings, Jonathan led Neziah from her parents' table to that of the king, and seated her there. His companions then seated themselves at the next table. The vast hall sighed, and the banquet was begun.

The wedding of Jonathan was celebrated for fourteen days, ceasing only for the rest on the Sabbath days. At last the guests began their homeward journeys, and the servants commenced to clean the remains of the festivities from the palace rooms. Michal was glad to be done with the wedding feast. She wanted to play, but each time she found a suitable spot she was chased away by busy servants.

A cool breeze met Michal as she exited to the wide, second story veranda overlooking the fields and mountains beyond. The servants had tidied and scrubbed here already, so the princess made her way to the chin high railing and leaned against it, watching the birds swoop and swirl above the fields in the valley below.

"Hello, small sister."

Michal started and turned to find Jonathan reclining behind her.

"You startled me, Jonathan," Michal said. She went to him and knelt, nestling against his prone form.

"Are you glad that the wedding festivities have ended?" the man asked the girl.

Michal put her arm around Jonathan's neck and rubbed her small cheek against his bearded one. "Yes."

A whole minute passed before Michal spoke again. She sat up and her brown eyes looked into Jonathan's deep blue ones.

"And will you now be the king in Father's place?"

A quick burst of laughter broke from Jonathan's lips, but he instantly sobered at Michal's injured expression. Very seriously he said, "No, dear princess. I will not become king until Father is very old. Then he will decide at what time I am to become king."

Michal relaxed her body against him again and entreated, "Tell me again how Father became the king."

Jonathan laughed his quick laughter again, and Michal smiled. "Father was seeking the donkeys that belonged to our grandfather. I was a boy, then, and I remember how concerned Grandfather and Uncle Ner were when the donkeys were found by others and brought back home and Father did not return. When Father did return several days later, he was a different man than the one who had left to seek the donkeys. The Spirit of the living God had come upon him and God had given him another heart. He told us that he had visited the great man of God, Samuel, and had been told that the donkeys were found already."

"All the tribes of Israel were called together to the Lord at Mizpeh by Samuel. There Samuel revealed to Israel that our father, Saul the son of Kish, had been chosen by the Lord to be their first king."

Jonathan paused, awaiting the question that Michal always asked. "And where was Father when they looked for him?"

"Hiding himself among the baggage!" exclaimed Jonathan, and they laughed together.[2]

Suddenly serious, Michal asked, "Did God choose Father to be the king because he is so handsome and so tall?"

Jonathan sobered also, but his eyes continued to smile at Michal. "I believe God chose our father for his humility and faith

---

[2]I Samuel 9:1-10:24

8

in the Lord.[3] Father is the tallest man in the kingdom,[4] but the Lord doesn't need anything in man himself to do His great work."

Michal pecked Jonathan's beard with a kiss. "I still love you, Jonathan, even though you are now married." She rose and ran back into the palace halls.

****

Michal loved Nob. There was the Tabernacle of the Lord, where blood was sacrificed in offerings to the Lord. Michal would lower her eyes when the lamb or bullock was slain beside the altar. But she loved the music of the trumpets which sounded at the sacrifices[5], the pungent odor of roasting flesh and ceremonial incense, and the great crowds of humanity. Way was always made for the king and his assemblage; however the press was usually enough to allow one small girl to slip away unnoticed for a moment or two, before retrieval by the tall black slave.

Michal had explored the environs of the Tabernacle as much as allowed during her previous visits. This time she darted quickly around a corner and knelt in a shadow, hoping to elude the watchful gaze of Zerah.

Crouched in concealment Michal gazed upon the city of Nob and the country beyond - wooded hills and luscious vales. She longed to break forth and climb among the trees on the hills, to roll in the grass beside the streams of water. But never had she done so, for hers was the life of proper decorum, a daughter of Saul, King of Israel.

"Hello."

Startled by a sudden voice, Michal tipped back on her

---

[3] I Samuel 9:21

[4] I Samuel 10:23

[5] Numbers 10:10

heels and fell seated in the dust. Before her stood a girl of about fifteen years. She wore a plain white linen dress, adorned only by a ribbon of blue upon the fringe.[6]

The girl knelt quickly beside Michal, helping her right herself and stand to her feet. Then, blushing, she bowed low before Michal and said in hushed excitement, "Forgive me, Princess!"

Michal rubbed her seat and frowned slightly. "How do you know who I am?"

"Your garments, Princess, betray you," the girl told her.

"My name is Michal, daughter of Saul," Michal said. "Who are you?"

"I am Jehoaddan, daughter of Ahimahaz, a priest of the Lord's Tabernacle."

Michal stared at Jehoaddan for a moment. "I have never spoken with one of a priest's family, before," she said finally.

"Nor I with a daughter of the king," replied Jehoaddan. Her dark eyes shone and Michal responded with a smile.

"It must be wondrous to be a daughter of the king," Jehoaddan said, "to live in a palace and have servants to wait upon your every whim."

Michal looked past the city walls to the hills beyond. "Have you ever climbed a hill or splashed through the waters of a stream?" she asked.

Jehoaddan followed her gaze and answered, "Yes."

"In my ten years I have not," Michal told her. "A princess must be guarded most carefully against anything improper. But I long so to do it."

"Perhaps one must accept the restrictions of one's station with grace, and be thankful for her lot in life," Jehoaddan said.

"Will you lead me through the gate of the city to the

---

[6]Numbers 15:38

hills?" Michal asked.

"Dear Princess, I must decline for I would not lead you astray. But I would like to be friends."

Michal frowned. "I would like to be friends, also. Please lead me to the gate of the city. I will make my own way to the hills."

Indecision played upon the features of Jehoaddan. Finally she sighed and said, "Very well. Come this way, Princess." She led through twisted streets past homes and behind the marketplace to a small wooden gate in the tall wall.

Michal's heart beat with anticipation. She would enter through that gate into a world she had only seen and never yet experienced. She flashed a smile at Jehoaddan. "Thank you," she said, and slipped quickly through the gate and into liberty.

"I will wait here for you, Princess," Jehoaddan called after her. "Do not be gone long. Please!" she implored.

Michal slipped down the steep hillside leading from the gate and took the path which followed the gentle curve of a glimmering stream. Flowers red, yellow and blue bobbed bright heads in the sun beside the footpath and under the shade of the trees. With her hands full of blossoms Michal pulled the sandals from her feet and splashed into the clear waters of the stream. She winced at her tender feet against the stones lining the bottom of the brook and stumbled a few steps before sitting against a moss covered rock. The fringe of her garment was wet before she could snatch it up, so she let it flow with the current. Pushing her toes into the stones beneath her feet, Michal watched tiny crabs scuttle away in alarm. She pushed her nose into the blossoms in her hand and drew their fragrance in slowly. Then, one by one she dropped the flowers onto the water and watched them boat away on the current. It was all that she had dreamed it would be. She smiled. The trees raised full green arms to wave to her. A flock of wooly clouds pranced across the heavens. The sun reached down with warm fingers and massaged her back and shoulders while the laughing waters tickled her feet. Somewhere a bird warbled its song to her.

A cool shadow fell, releasing the sun's embrace and she knew that her dream was finished, her rapture shattered. She bowed her head and felt the tears burning behind her eyes, but they did not burn through. Lifting her chin she turned to face the tall black slave.

"Come, Princess," Zerah intoned severely. But Michal saw a secret smile playing about his lips. Jehoaddan stood near the gate of the city, twisting her hands nervously. Michal put her sandals upon her wet feet, and holding her head high, preceded the slave up the hillside.

"Oh, Princess!" Jehoaddan cried when she had reached the gate. "Will you be in terrible trouble?" She looked intently into Zerah's black eyes and pleaded, "It was my fault. I led her to the gate."

Michal watched Zerah. The smile had submerged completely now, but his eyes danced. "The princess is needed," was all that he said. Then he turned and stood waiting for Michal.

Michal smiled broadly at Jehoaddan and said, "I will remember this day always. I hope that we meet again." Then she strode dutifully toward the Tabernacle, followed by Zerah.

****

The servants hushed when entering a room. Michal and Merab remained inside, with no explanation. At the order of Ziba, head steward, their meals were delivered. Their tutor brought the scrolls and volumes to their rooms and there they were schooled. A stout old servant woman, turning sideways to clear the doorway, brought the brightly colored strands for embroidery. The sisters sat near an open window, the sunshine warming their heads and backs, bent over their needlework.

"Do you know?" Merab asked without looking up.

"Know?" asked Michal, pricking her finger as she looked

up. Into her mouth it went to staunch the flow of blood. A girl of fourteen years must not stain her embroidery.

"What happened to father in the land of the Amalekites," Merab answered.

"No," said Michal, laying her embroidery into her lap. "Do you?"

Merab nodded.

"Tell me."

"The Prophet Samuel gave Father a message from the Lord God. The Lord told Father to destroy the Amalekites, because they had done wrong to Israel long ago." Her eyes did not leave her work, and her stitches were even and straight.

"And did he?" Michal asked impatiently.

"He did. But he and his soldiers saved alive the king and the best of the sheep and oxen." Merab stitched silently for a moment.

"Merab," Michal chided.

Merab now looked up from her work and Michal saw tears spilling down her cheeks. "The Prophet Samuel told Father that because he has rejected the Lord, the Lord has rejected him from being the king. Samuel told him that the Lord has torn the kingdom of Israel from him and given it to a neighbor of his that is better than he."[7]

"Then is Father no longer the king?" Michal asked, rising to her feet, her embroidery falling to the floor.

"I don't know," Merab told her. "I suppose that we are secluded as this because of what happened. Perhaps we'll have to leave the palace."

Michal ran across the room and pushed past Zerah into the hallway. Quick steps carried her to the lower chambers, where she found her mother clutching Jonathan, both in tears.

---

[7] I Samuel 15

She knew something was terribly wrong. She threw her arms around them both and cried, "My father! My father is no longer king!"

CHAPTER 2

THE PRINCESS AND THE SHEPHERD

"He chose David also his servant, and took him from the sheepfolds." Psalm 78:70

The queen pulled the princess away and led her aside. She looked sternly at Michal. "You are to be in your rooms." Michal looked hopelessly into her mother's eyes. "Merab told me what happened to Father," she wept. "Must we leave our home, Mother?"

The confusion clouding her mother's face cleared and she nodded slightly. "I see," she said. "No, Michal, we must not leave our home. Your father is the king as he ever has been."

Michal looked toward her grieving brother. "Why are you and Jonathan distressed?"

The queen closed her eyes and sighed. "This is not the business of children," she said. She sighed again and put her arm around Michal's shoulders. "Jonathan's child was born this morning, but he lived only an hour."

Michal returned to her rooms. Her heart ached for the loss of Jonathan's child, a strange ache she had never before known. Yet the fear had dissolved. Father was yet the king of Israel.

A strangeness pervaded the palace home of the king. Life resumed its usual course, but Michal felt the burden daily. Her father fell often into deep depressions, and occasional fits of violence. Michal saw her brothers leave the king's dining hall in haste one day, escorting their wives quickly away. She followed Jonathan to the broad gardens of the palace. Neziah stood beside him, pale and silent.

"What happened?" Michal asked, grasping her brother's arm. "Why do you all leave this way?"

Jonathan spoke quietly to his wife, and she sat to wait,

clutching her hands in her lap, her knuckles blanching.

"It is our father," Jonathan told Michal. His long flowing robe formed a tent about her as he circled her with his arm. "He is not himself lately. Often." A great sadness shadowed Jonathan's features. "Tonight at table he became violent and we feared for the lives of our wives. For our own lives." Jonathan hung his head and Michal felt his weight against her shoulders.

At fourteen years of age, Michal was tall and sturdy, yet Jonathan leaned heavily upon her and she spoke with difficulty, "Is it because our father disobeyed the Lord?"

"I fear it is," Jonathan said. When he lifted his eyes to meet Michal's, she saw a depth of sorrow flowing from his grieving heart. "It is as if the Lord has taken His Spirit from him, and has left an evil spirit to trouble him."[8] Jonathan turned his sorrowful eyes toward Neziah, beckoning her.

Jonathan gave Michal a final squeeze and followed by servants walked to his rooms of the palace.

A dread clutched and pressed her heart, but Michal had no fear of her father. She entered the throne room and was blinded by the bright fingers of sunlight filtering through the high window to the right of the throne. Tiny specks of dust, like minuscule worlds, floated through the golden tendrils of light. Against the brilliance the untouched reaches of the room lurked dark and forbidding, their colors and richness obscured.

Michal approached the throne and bowed herself low before the seated majesty.

"Michal," her father said simply.

Michal rose and mounted the steps to the throne. Standing beside the throne she reached across the ornate graven armrest to embrace her father. He held her firmly against him and she stood in silence beside the king.

"All is not well with your father, Princess," Saul said

---

[8]I Samuel 16:14

gravely.

"Can I aid you, Father?" Michal asked.

The creases of care relaxed from Saul's dark, handsome face. He smiled at his youngest child. "Your very presence aids me, child. I fear that nothing can cure me." The king gazed at Michal for a moment. When he again spoke, his tone was confiding, serious. "What think you, Michal? Shall I call a musician to calm my troubled spirit?" Michal was unsure if she were to answer the question.

Saul leaned forward with his elbows upon his knees, watching the flecks drift in the shafted light. "One has suggested a shepherd boy. It is said he is cunning with the harp and lute, and to be desired for prudence and valor." Saul straightened and looked back into Michal's eyes. "And the Lord is with him," he said in a hushed voice.

Saul sat silently, watching Michal. She reached her hand to stroke his smooth, soft beard, as she had when a small child seated on his lap. "Yes, Father. Do try the musician. I want so for you to be well."

"Then it is done," said the king, leaning back against the cushions of his throne and closing his eyes, thus dismissing the princess.

The sky hung low and threatened a storm the day of the musician's arrival. A great flurry preceded him to the throne room. Michal and Merab peered through the myriad of plants lining the hallway, behind which they concealed themselves.

Michal's father had said that he was a shepherd boy, but the young man who passed them was not at all as she had expected. Tall, although not as tall as the king, he was bronzed from sun and wind. Sturdy arms emerged from his rugged dress, clenching a small wooden harp, and solid legs propelled his way. A tumble of rusty curls framed a strong face, with wide set eyes and a square jaw. The shepherd musician moved with confidence and determination, although it was apparent that he was in unaccustomed environs.

"Oooh!" Merab exclaimed after the entourage had passed.

"What is his name?" Michal whispered fiercely.

"David," Merab answered, a touch of reverence coloring the word. "He lives in Bethlehem. Isn't he splendid!"

Michal looked at her sister in disdain. "He's a shepherd boy, Merab."

Merab's answer was in the same reverent tone, "Yes."

The whole of the palace quieted to hear the song of the shepherd boy. It lifted from his lips to kiss the rafters of the throne room and wafted through the walls to permeate to the farthest corner. All labour ceased. Every ear was tuned to the delicate shape and texture of the music. The heart of each was carried away on arms of melody to distant memories of places and times. When the last notes had waned and ebbed away on the afternoon breeze, sighs filled the stone halls and chambers of the palace as subjects and sovereign alike returned to the present.

Merab leaned against the wall, limp and faint. "I have never heard a more beautiful sound. Surely, if anything exists to cure our father, it is the music of David."

Michal, too, reposed against the cold, hard stones, had felt the awe of the music. Her heart thumped within her breast as a wild beast endeavoring escape. The musicians of the palace were the finest to be had, yet this simple shepherd boy had outsung them all.

"I am sure that Father found his song refreshing," Merab said. "I am so glad that he will be staying in the palace."

Michal scowled at Merab and clucked disapproval. "He's but a shepherd, Merab. Mind your place." But Michal's heart smiled, too, that David would stay.

The storm broke in fury just as the servants began to clear away the evening repast. Saul and Ahinoam, with their married sons and wives, retired to a chamber filled with comforts and color. A fire blazed upon the hearth and each one seated himself upon large, downy cushions. Servants bustled about to see to the comfort of each, and then melted into the shadows to wait summons.

Michal and Merab, escorted to their rooms, were gloomy and listless. "David will give concert this evening," Merab whined mournfully. "Oh that we, too, could be there."

Michal rose to her feet and confronted the tall black slave who guarded the door. "Zerah, take us to the king."

Zerah smiled, showing glistening teeth against his dark features. "You were sent to your rooms, your majesty."

"Yes," Michal said impatiently, "but we now desire to hear the musician." She looked toward Merab. "We are no longer children. Merab is old enough to marry. We will soon take our meals with our parents." Michal's haughty tone dissolved to pleading. "Please, Zerah, take us to the king."

Zerah's smile vanished. "You wish that I be flogged for your pleasure, Princess?"

"I will protect you. You will not be harmed. Only take us to the king."

Zerah led the two excited girls to the hall outside the chamber. He did not seek admittance, but folded his arms and stood before the door. Thankful to be at the door the girls did not press the man to take them inside, but instead crowded closely to the thick cedar planks.

A cramp was stealing into Michal's legs from her awkward posture when the strings of the harp were finally plucked and the remarkable voice of David lifted on the evening air. Punctuated by thunderclaps his song rose and fell as the ebb and flow of the sea. His very words escaped Michal, but his music embraced her, warm, secure, stable. She closed her eyes and was lost to time and place as her soul was swept to dimensions of the heart alone. How could a mortal tongue lisp so sweetly the strain of heaven?

Michal revived to the gentle nudge of the black slave. She stood on stiff legs and submissively followed Merab back to their rooms. Merab sat upon her bed and wept softly.

"Have you ever heard such beauty?" she asked Michal.

Michal knew that they had been witness to a miracle.

Daily the king would call his shepherd musician to the throne room. Daily the household would pause to the ecstacy of David's song. The name of David graced the lips of many conversations. Merab sat for hours, staring out a window, handwork lying untouched in her lap, sighing at the thought of David. But when her heart rose to her lips and she spoke his name, Michal would scowl. As often as the name of David was spoken between them, Merab was reminded brusquely of her station in life.

The king delighted in the young man. He was pleased to have David in tow as he went about his majestic duties. David accompanied Saul to survey the troops, bearing Saul's armour as well as the ever present harp. Kneeling upon the ground beneath a towering tree, David would sing and play to ease Saul's troubled soul. The soldiers of Israel stood their ground obediently, but eyes and ears sought the young shepherd musician. As he walked about the encampment many nods and greetings met him from smiling faces. David met each one with a quick smile and returned greeting.

David was singing again for her father, and Michal stole into the throne room, hiding in its shadows. Saul sat upon his throne, his arms stretched upon the armrests and his hands clutching the ornate gold. His head was bowed low, and his body trembled. David knelt before him, softly brushing the strings of his harp. David's eyes were closed and his face was raised to the heavens. Michal could distinguish his words as he sang, and she listened intently, hungrily.

"The LORD is my shepherd; I shall not want.
He maketh me to lie down in green pastures:
He leadeth me beside the still waters.
He restoreth my soul: he leadeth me in the paths of
    righteousness for his name's sake.
Yea, though I walk through the valley of the shadow of
    death,

I will fear no evil: for thou art with me; thy rod and thy staff they comfort me.

Thou preparest a table before me in the presence of mine enemies:

Thou anointest my head with oil; my cup runneth over

Surely goodness and mercy shall follow me all the days of my life:

And I will dwell in the house of the LORD for ever."[9]

The melody was sweet and haunting, but the words gripped Michal's heart. She had never heard so tender and intimate utterance about the Lord. It was a prayer set to music. This shepherd boy, David, surely knew the Lord in a way foreign to Michal. And she, the princess, envied the shepherd boy.

Later that week the women of the royal family sat upon stone benches, wrapped only in large linen towels. The air was already oppressive with heat, but as the sluice was released and the cold waters flowed around and over the heated stones, a fine mist of steam rose around them further compressing the air. The fog obscured all vision, but the women in the tiny room spoke with each other through the mists in mild tones. Michal listened to her mother and sisters in law and frequently heard the name of David spoken. Merab reached through the vapors and nudged Michal at the sound of his name. Since her face could not be seen, Michal did not bother to wear her habitual scowl, but hissed in reply, "Sister!"

Neziah was speaking and Michal heard, "O, that Jonathan were here at the palace instead of with the armies at Michmash. I know that he would admire the music of David." There was a pause and then Neziah added, "And the person as well."

After they had perspired sufficiently, the women departed to a large room to unveil and plunge beneath the tepid waters of

---

[9]Psalm 23:1-6

the bathing pool. Michal drifted and floated, sometimes diving to the smooth plastered bottom, to pop to the surface and startle Merab or one of the sisters in law.

Michal then stretched herself upon a flat couch, once again robed with a towel, to be rubbed with olive oil and perfumes. Her long, thick hair was plaited in numerous ropes and these were all carefully wound about her head, ending in a pile high above her brow. Soft garments were laid against her skin and covered with a gown of bright blue. In final touch, a servant held out her many colored robe for her to don.

Her toilet complete, Michal wandered from the company of the women, leaving the pleasant chatter and fragrant aromas behind. Her skin fairly glowing from the buffing she had received, she climbed to the broad veranda overlooking the beauty of this land flowing with milk and honey.

Sun beams played among the foliage of the grand sycamore tree which edged the palace. Michal was at eye level with its upper branches and eagerly noticed a bird's nest, concealed in a deep crevice between two stout limbs. She watched with interest as a parent winged to the nest's edge bearing a meal, thrusting it into a baby bird's gaping mouth.

So absorbed was she in the aviary display that the sudden strain of music and the mellow tones of voice jolted her. She started in alarm and pivoted to find David, kneeling in song on the far end of the veranda.

Suddenly shy to hear his devotions undisclosed, she tried to glide to the door unnoticed. But as soon as she moved, the music stopped. David rose to his feet and approached her, kneeling on one knee before her, head bowed.

"Forgive me, Princess," he said. "I did not mean to disturb you. I thought I was alone here."

Why did Michal's skin begin to burn? Why did her heart thump so that she could hear it in her ears? Why should her knees suddenly wobble and threaten collapse? Why did she, the princess, feel that she should be the one prostrate before the shepherd?

Placing her hands against her hot cheeks, which she guessed were also crimson, she breathed deeply, seeking to regain her composure.

"You did not disturb me," she answered, amazed that her voice was even.

David then looked up at her, still kneeling, and she was astonished at the blueness of his eyes and how they smiled at her. His copper colored hair fell about his face in unruly coils, yet he looked not the least disheveled. Clothed in soft garments given him by the king, David looked every bit a prince.

When Michal withdrew her eyes from his to gaze into the horizon, she wondered how long their eyes had locked thus in silence.

Coming fully to her senses, Michal saw that David still knelt, his large form bent low, balancing on one knee. "You may rise," she told him.

As he unfolded himself to stand, he towered over her, although Michal herself was quite tall.

"Shall I play for you?" David asked, extending his harp toward her.

"No," Michal said, quite abruptly. "Thank you. I must go." David bowed from the waist and she hurried away, feeling his eyes watch her through the doorway. She closed the door behind her and leaned against the wall. Her heart once again pounded wildly. Never in all of her fourteen years had she fawned before a servant, a mere subject of her father's realm. And why should she not have let him play for her? His music gave her much pleasure. Her heart could not answer, and she suddenly fled to her rooms lest the comely shepherd musician depart and see her there.

******* ***

Michal pushed past the attendants and statesmen in the

throne room to her father's side. Even the sweet music of David had not soothed his troubled soul this day. The Philistines, a fierce and strong people, had gathered their armies on a mountain above the Valley of Elah to battle the armies of Israel. Saul stood before his throne barking orders to his captains and they hastened away to ready the troops for war. Saul's Uncle Abner, the general of his armies, was ordered to fetch Jonathan and the troops with him to the Valley of Elah.

Michal bowed before the king, then mounted the steps and embraced him tenderly. She knew that her father feared war. The Lord was no longer with him, and he could no longer rest assured that the armies of Israel would prevail against the enemy. She desired to comfort him, but there was no solace.

"Ah, Michal," the king said, pulling her to him. "And what do you think, small princess? Will the armies of the Lord defeat the dreaded Philistines?"

Michal had no answer, so she stretched her arm to stroke the soft beard and smile at her father.

The women of the palace stood upon the wide balcony and watched Saul lead his soldiers toward the Valley of Elah. Sorrow pressed on every heart. Battles always claim a toll, without respect of lineage or rank. But the eyes of Michal followed a solitary figure which made its way along a path toward the south. David had been sent by Saul back to his father in Bethlehem, back to his sheep.

Merab, too, watched the lonely retreating figure. "Do you suppose we will ever see David again?" she sighed wistfully.

Michal gripped the low wall of the balcony, leaning forward over it. Closing her eyes she said softly, "Perhaps it is better if he does not return. A princess must keep her heart for better things." Both girls watched him turn as he topped the rise and wave briefly back toward the palace. Then he was gone.

All inhabitants of Gibeah awaited anxiously the messengers from the camp on the mountain overlooking the Valley of Elah, across from the terrible Philistines. Every day a strong runner left the tent of Saul to carry news to the palace. He brought personal news to the queen and the wives of Saul's sons. Yet, the accounts of the battle were peculiar. An arrow had yet to be shot from either army. No spear had been thrown. Alas, no blood had been shed, and for this the women were deeply grateful. What did take place at the yet to be battle ground was curious. Every day a massive soldier of the Philistine army presented himself to the men of Israel and made challenge to them. He offered to the armies of Israel their liberty if but one man would meet him alone in combat, and defeat him. For over thirty days the runners had delivered the same message: No one had answered the giant's challenge.

CHAPTER 3

THE PRINCESS AND THE CHAMPION

"The right hand of the LORD is exalted: the right hand of the
LORD doeth valiantly." Psalm 118:16

The women of the family royal travelled to the hill city of
Nob to offer sacrifices before the Lord and pray for the
triumph of Israel. As was her custom when in the city of
the priests, Michal sought the fellowship of Jehoaddan.

Long beams of late afternoon sun dappled through the
branches overhead as the two young women walked through a
grove of olive trees and bowed beneath the branches to sit upon
a gnarled root. They found comfort in each other, these two
from so different worlds.

"I am so happy for you," Michal said. "I would that I
could attend your wedding feast." She paused and looked across
the hillside to the brook to which she had escaped when a child.
With a sigh she said, "But we wait anxiously each day for word
from the Valley of Elah. Three of my brothers are there with my
father. We came here only in the need to petition the Lord."

"I, too, wish that you could be present when Mahli and
I are wed," said Jehoaddan. A soft blush brushed her cheek, and
she lowered her eyes shyly. "But I understand your distress.
Such strange things are heard from Elah."

"And news that has shattered my sister," Michal told her.
"The runner who last brought us tidings before we left for Nob
brought a message from my father. The King has promised to
the man who will meet and conquer the giant great riches and the

25

hand of his elder daughter in marriage."[10] Michal looked into Jehoaddan's wide eyes. "Merab is grieving. She fears he will be old, ugly, and cruel."

"The man who slays the mighty adversary of the Lord's army must needs be a man of courage and power," Jehoaddan told her. "A man so brave, whatever his age and appearance, could not have a cruel heart."

"You are so good, Jehoaddan," Michal smiled at her. "Merab is noble, yet she desires more than a virtuous heart in a husband."

"The Lord will give her the grace to accept what she must," Jehoaddan said quietly.

The two friends, bound in understanding, sat in silence upon the hillside of Israel, and let their thoughts flow unimpeded by words.

****

Emotions raged against one another in Michal's heart. The Philistine giant, for so long the terror of the armies of the Lord, had been slain. Palace bards told and retold the story. The visiting brother of a soldier, a mere boy, clad only in rough shepherd's garb and armed with a sling and five stones, had defeated the foe before whom the valiant of Israel had trembled with fear.

All palace faces smiled, from the parlour to the kitchen. All hearts were warmed, for the champion of Israel was their own musician, David. His name had ever come easily to palace lips since his arrival, but it rose ever more frequently, now. Servants who had received a word from David during his sojourn there boasted to one another, embellishing each account,

---

[10] I Samuel 17:25

claiming conversance with the hero of Israel.

Merab's rapture was unbounded. She drifted about the palace buoyed by joy. She was to be the wife of David! It had been decreed by her father, the King of Israel. David was no longer a shepherd, beneath her station and unworthy of a princess. He was a warrior courageous and noble, renowned in all the land for his valiant feat in killing Goliath. Her happiness enveloped her. She did not see the face of her younger sister. She could not detect the anguish of Michal's heart. Merab's was a misery transformed into bliss.

But Michal's heart indeed knew pain. Not for her sister; for Merab no longer suffered. Michal's agony was her own. She had known before his departure that David held her heart. His leaving had left her heart aching, empty. But she had hoped to secretly dream of David for a lifetime, needing never to know what befell him. But now David would wed her sister. David would be her brother in law. She must see him often, speak with him, watch him with Merab, and never let either know of her love for him.

David's legend grew until he himself was in every way a giant. As the days passed following the great victory of Israel over the Philistines the palace was festive in anticipation of the return of the king and the troops of Israel to Gibeah.

Michal and Merab crowded together to peer out the window of their room. The streets below were a mass of humanity, thronging in great surges toward the gate of the city. Every flat rooftop held a company of enthusiastic spectators awaiting the triumphant return of the troops.

Soldiers astride tall steeds coaxed the multitudes back along the edges of the cobbled street, making way for the warriors. They found it necessary to dismount and line the horses sideways along the route, stretching arms out full to restrain the excited throngs. Yet, a band of women escaped the restrictions, and tambourines in hand, danced along the street before the advancing armies. Their chant drifted above the clamour of the crowds below to the ears of the two girls observing from the window. Just as the king appeared, with the hero, David, at his side, these words wafted to them.

"Saul has killed his thousands. David has killed his ten thousands!"[11]

The joyful chant was reiterated and echoed as the army advanced.

"Listen!" Merab exulted. "They praise their champion." She looked into the sky dreamily, and whispered, "My husband!"

Michal frowned, but not at Merab's joy. She sorrowed for her father. He rode into his city a victorious monarch, and his subjects praised David more than him. Saul was a proud man. Michal knew these words would wound his heart, bruise his very soul.

As the victors neared the palace, Michal saw with horror that David clutched in his right hand a morbid trophy, the head of the giant, Goliath. It was a spectacular prize, she knew, for it proved the demise of the adversary of God's people. He held it aloft and a cheer arose anew.

When the grand assemblage of the king entered the palace courtyard, Michal and Merab descended the stairs. Merab, whose feet barely touched the floor, drifted along in a dream. She saw David only. Michal, however, noticed that David wore the garments of her brother, Jonathan. Strapped to his back was the quiver of Jonathan. As he dismounted and handed the ghastly trophy to a servant, Michal saw him detach both the sword and bow of Jonathan from the horse's saddle. Her heart leapt. Had Jonathan been lost in the battle? Why should David have his effects?

Michal pushed through the servants assembled in greeting to the king to stand at his side.

---

[11] I Samuel 18:7

"Father!" she exclaimed, embracing him. "Where is Jonathan?" She gazed at David accusingly. He smiled at her and then glanced past her, nodding. She was suddenly chagrined as she turned to see Jonathan embracing Neziah. She glanced shyly toward David and smiled timidly. Then she walked beside her father's tall form toward her sister and the waiting queen.

A grand banquet was served to celebrate the return of Michal's father and brothers, and the giant slayer dined with them at the king's table. Michal and Merab, now considered grown and fit to dine with their parents, sat silently, listening intently to the accounts of the men. David ate quietly, smiling at each one who addressed him, answering without bravado. Merab's eyes never left David's face. Michal, however, watched the shadows pass over her father's handsome features at the obvious admiration of David.

With the repast ended, Michal followed Jonathan and drew him aside privately. She searched his fair face. "I am so glad to have you home," she told him, embracing him briefly and planting a soft kiss upon his beard. Then she examined him again, asking suddenly, "Why does David wear your robe and bear your sword and bow?"

"David," Jonathan said, satisfaction coloring the word. "I have never known a man such as he before. With no fear, only confident faith in the Lord, he faced Goliath with a stone and a sling. He never doubted that victory would be his. I have never known a man to love God as David does, nor to simply trust the Lord so fully." Jonathan paused, his eyes looking at her, but his mind far away. Then he smiled and said, "I have covenanted myself to David for life. The robe and weapons were tokens of my admiration." He paused again and then said, in hushed tones, "I have never known such a man!"

The maidens in charge of the toilet of the two young women worked deftly with skilled hands to sculpt hair and adorn with beautiful jewels. Michal, however, reprimanded them for their sluggishness. David would again give concert, as was his habit when only a shepherd musician, and this time Merab and Michal would sit with their parents, brothers and sisters in law in the music salon. As the final touch was laid upon Michal's hair, Merab pulled her from her stool and led her from the room to the broad staircase which descended to the main hall. Zerah stepped quickly to escort the princesses down the stairs and to the salon door. There he stepped inside and melted into the shadows near the door, arms folded across his chest.

Merab's eyes shone as she lighted upon a cushion, never taking her eyes from the face of David. Michal sat beside her, warmed by the secret of her love for David, pained in the knowledge of its hopelessness.

David knelt close to King Saul, bowing his head in silent prayer. With his lifted head came the mellow tones of his voice and the sweet strain of the harp. Michal tore her eyes from his still beardless face, lifted in rapturous song, and gazed at her family around her. Merab, of course, was lost in ecstacy. Neziah's lips curled slightly in pleasure, and Jonathan leaned his elbows forward upon his knees, elation upon his fair features. The queen's head was tilted slightly to the side, and she, too, smiled softly. But when her eyes rested upon the face of her father, Michal's heart cringed in alarm. His handsome features were distorted in turbulence. The black brows frowned until they met above his eyes, stormy in their blackness. Through his beard Michal detected the corners of his mouth drawn into a deep scowl. He alone in the room was not contented at the hearing of David's song.

Michal could scarcely sleep for the memory of her father's gloominess. He was just returned from the great battle with the Philistines, but she feared he was tormented already with the evil spirit which afflicted him.

Michal and Merab sat upon the terrace, breaking their fast upon fruits and nectar. The sun had risen only a short time before, and already David had been summoned to the throne room to relieve the king's deep depression. Michal remembered the foregoing evening and puzzled whether the music would bring a cure in the fresh morning air.

A sudden crash and shout brought both princesses to their feet in alarm. Angry curses issued from the throne room and quick steps hastened there from all over the palace. Michal and Merab arrived, breathless, just as David slipped out the doorway, great dismay in his wide eyes.

Jonathan appeared, and clutching David's arms asked in dread what had happened.

David looked into his companion's eyes, hesitant to reveal the truth. "I'm alright," he said, speaking slowly, cautiously. "My music couldn't tame the wild beast within your father, today."

"What happened, David?" Jonathan demanded kindly.

Not able to avoid the revelation, David lowered his eyes and spoke quietly. "The king threw a javelin at me as I played."[12]

Jonathan sighed and closed his eyes for a moment. Then, probing David's eyes with his own he said, "It was the wild beast within him which hurled the spear at you, David, not Saul." He held David's gaze until the younger man nodded, and then Jonathan released his grip. The two men walked away down the corridor together, silently.

"But David and I are to be betrothed," Merab wailed to Michal on an afternoon soon after.

Michal wished to comfort her sister, but to assure her of her coming marriage to David was difficult for her. Saul had not yet spoken to David of Merab, and David would now be sent from the palace to become captain over a troop of a thousand men.

Michal sat beside Merab, searching for words. "I am sure that David will return, soon, and then Father will fulfill his promise," she told her. She closed her eyes and softly repeated,

---

[12]   I Samuel 18:10,11

"I am sure."

The evening before David was to report to his new post as captain, the king was again in turmoil with the spirit which tormented him. David was summoned and played a final song to ease Saul. But again the music failed to accomplish its purpose. In the sight of the attending servants, the queen, and Abner the general of the armies of Israel, Saul seized a javelin and once again attempted to take David's life.

No vindication was made for the king's action, and David departed early the next morning for the encampment of Israel.

The dust of Merab's crumbled dreams settled about her sadly. Her fair young face was drawn and somber. Her words were seldom spoken without melting into sobs of despair.

"Michal!" she would cry, wringing her slender hands and casting her gaze about her hopelessly. "Father has sent David away without a word of our betrothal!" Her large liquid eyes bright with tears would then beseech Michal's. "What if I should lose him, Michal? I could not bear it!"

Not a day passed but the name of David was spoken in awe and reverence by the men of Israel and Judah. Unaware of the king's disdain of Israel's hero, callers at the palace, as well as emissaries from the troops, spoke their admiration for the valiant soldier. Saul's vexation increased until the heaviness of his displeasure weighed upon all who loved him.

Michal found her father pacing before his throne, angry gestures stabbing at the air, face set deeply in a scowl. She approached slowly, unafraid, yet wary.

"Father," she said softly.

Saul stopped still and looked toward her. He reached out an arm and folded her against him. She felt him tremble and reached to stroke his beard which was moist with bitter tears.

"Father," she repeated.

When he spoke his voice was thick with anguish. "My people, my kingdom. They love him."

"You are their king, Father. Your people love you,"

Michal cooed, as to soothe a weeping child.

"I am their king," Saul mourned. "But they love David." He released her and returned to his pacing.

Michal sat upon the queen's throne and watched him. She had not come to discuss the kingdom, but her love for Merab had compelled her to speak to Saul of David. The pain gnashed at her heart cruelly, but David could not be hers, and it was Merab's right to wed him. So she spoke, the words falling dully before her, but stabbing her sharply.

"Father, did you not make a promise to the armies of Israel, that he who would slay the giant Goliath would be given the hand of your elder daughter?" She paused, watching him falter in his stride. "Merab wishes for you to fulfill that promise."

Saul halted and turned his sorrowful eyes to her. "Does Merab love him, too?"

Michal stood before him, looking up into his turbulent eyes. "Yes, Father. And she desires that you fulfill your promise."

Her father stared at her for a moment. She watched the muscles of his handsome face relax, and a subtle smile began to play about his mouth. His eyes seemed to study her carefully and when he spoke his voice was soft and almost merry.

"Yes, Yes," he said. "The King of Israel must not fail to keep such a promise. Tell your sister that I will send for David immediately."

Saul's sudden swing in mood astonished the noble family, but Merab's elation returned in full. David was summoned from the army, and he knelt before the king in the throne room. A beam of sunlight fell upon him from the tall window and lit his bronzed features, illumining his copper hair with golden lights. Michal's breath caught at the spectacle.

David remained prone before him as Saul's voice resounded against the high ceiling in majesty. "You did your people a great service in killing the Philistine giant. The King of Israel gave his pledge that he who would free Israel from her foe would have the hand of his daughter in marriage." Saul paused and then intoned gravely, "Rise."

David stood before him, his square jaw set firmly, his sapphire eyes fairly sparkling in the radiant light.

Michal sensed her father falter ever so briefly at the man who stood before him. But his voice was steady as he gestured toward Merab and spoke. "Behold my elder daughter, Merab. I will give her to you as your wife."

David fell to his knees again, bowing low before the king. His words were muffled, but Michal heard him say, "Who am I? What is my life, or my father's family in Israel, that I should be a son in law to the king?"

Michal detected the subtle smile spread over her father's face. His voice rang regally when he spoke, "Only be valiant for me, David, and fight the Lord's battles."[13]

David returned to the troops of Israel betrothed to Merab, daughter of Saul, King of Israel. Merab sat each day in the sunshine, the beams of light glinting against the gold of her hair, and embroidered beauty into the bodice of her wedding gown, creating a delicate web of lace for her veil. She blushed with pleasure at each remembrance of her coming wedding to David, the magnificent champion of Israel.

Michal watched Merab's happiness darkly. The close fellowship the girls had shared through the years was severed by Merab's immersion in her own joy, which Michal could not share.

Jonathan found his sisters thus one afternoon on the veranda.

He smiled toward Merab, but spoke to Michal. "She is happy." He looked out across the verdant fields. "I am happy, too, Michal, and thankful to the Lord that David will be my brother." A cloud passed over Jonathan's fair face, and he frowned slightly. "Our father is hard to be understood, Michal."

---

[13]I Samuel 18:17,18

He looked into her eyes, a doubt deep behind the smile in his blue ones. "You know that Father twice attempted to slay David." He shook his head as if to clear the thought away. "And yet he has promised his daughter in marriage to David." His smile returned. "And David, my friend, will be David, my brother."

***** ***

Jonathan paced the stones impatiently, wringing his hands helplessly. Merab and Michal were both full old enough, now, to witness the birth of Jonathan's child. However, Michal preferred to take the excursions from the birthing room to Jonathan to report on the progress. Perspiration wet the fair hair of Jonathan's brow and his yellow beard. His tunic stuck to his back. Michal knew that tears were mingled with the streaks of sweat upon Jonathan's distressed features. He had lost his first child at birth, and once again Neziah struggled to bring forth a child. The weary hours had expired without progress, and even the finest physicians in Saul's kingdom could not make Jonathan's child come to birth.

King Saul, who had not paid much mind to the birth of his previous grandchildren, awaited with Jonathan the possible heir to the throne of Israel. Michal could give no word of encouragement, but she embraced the weary form of her brother and let him weep against her.

"I have prayed," he told her. "I have asked the Lord to let this child be born. If only David were here, I would ask him to pray, also. He knows God so intimately." Michal glanced at her father and saw the shadow cross his face.

All eyes turned to the door as the queen entered the room bearing a bundle in her arms. She crossed to Jonathan, handing the blanketed form to him, seating him and herself at his side, embracing her son as he wept over the still, silent form of the son who would never be king of Israel.

****

According to custom, the wedding feast was provided by the bridegroom, or his family. However, the wedding of Merab to David would be celebrated at the palace in Gibeah. A date was set and messengers rode the invitation to the wedding to the far reaches of Saul's kingdom. A special envoy took a letter from the hand of the king to the parents and family of David in Bethlehem.

The palace was buzzing with activity. The steward, Ziba, shouted instructions in every direction. Servants bustled about importantly, each knowing that his part in the preparations could determine that the wedding of David proceeded smoothly. The palace confectioners created mountains of delicacies. The finest beasts and fowl were selected to be roasted for the banquet.

Almost all in the palace were happy about the coming festivities, from the royal family to the lowest servant. Saul, however, strolled in solitary, flanked at a distance by his guards. He traversed hill and valley, returning to the palace in the purple dusk to sulk alone in his throne room. His seething silence would be broken occasionally by a burst of outrage at the report of a messenger from the troops of Israel captained by David. Michal pondered his fury, wondering.

Merab's pleasure spilled out about her, infecting her mother, her maidens, the servants who ministered to her. Only Michal was immune to her bliss. Merab would never know, could never know. She would be David's wife and live in supreme happiness. Michal would see them together and would suffer in utter misery.

David had not yet returned to Gibeah. Dignitaries from the twelve tribes arrived at the palace in great pomp and were assigned to apartments within its grand dimensions. Vendors hawked their wares loudly before the palace gate, descending upon each new arrival in fervor.

A great flock of servant women hovered about Merab the

morning of her wedding. She emerged the image of loveliness, her embroidered white gown sweeping gracefully to the polished floor, her golden tresses piled high above her brow, the delicate veil concealing her fair features.

She broke away from the attentions of the maid servants and clutched Michal's arm anxiously. "Have you seen David?" she queried, concern etching her voice sharply. "Is he yet in the palace?" Michal cooed comfort to her. Of course David must be in the palace. The wedding feast was to take place at the noon hour. No, she had not seen him, but there was no cause for alarm. Surely David would attend his own wedding.

A sharp knock sounded at the door. Zerah opened to the king, himself, who quickly entered the chamber and motioned the servants to exit. Zerah followed the flurry of women, closing the door behind him. Michal stood at Merab's side, a premonition of disaster gnawing at her heart, watching her father closely.

"Merab, my beauty!" he exclaimed. He walked around her, surveying the image before him, and then stopped to face her. "You are far too great a prize for your father to give lightly," he said. The tiny doubt continued to gnaw at Michal's heart. "I have determined a greater position for you than that which was previously arranged." Merab's eyes widened in confusion, and Michal's heart pounded wildly. Saul smiled at Merab and spoke lightly, joyfully. "Adriel the Meholathite has wrought great deeds for me in the battles of Israel," he said. "I would reward him, and what greater prize than the hand of my elder daughter in marriage?"[14]

"Father!" Merab gasped. "I am to wed David today."

Saul waved the words away. "I have decided." He turned and walked to the door, turning before leaving the room to say, "You are a vision of loveliness, Merab. Until the feast."

Silence reigned as the moments elapsed. Michal was

---

[14] I Samuel 18:19

faint, her mind a maze of confusion, yet she knew that Merab would need her aid. She reached for Merab's arm and felt her tremble. Then, suddenly, Merab gave a sharp cry and was in a heap upon the floor.

"Zerah, come!" Michal called, kneeling beside the prostrate form of Merab. The black slave lifted the princess gently and placed her upon a bed. Then he stepped away, keeping his eyes upon the drawn face of the elder princess.

Michal knelt at her side, shaking her gently, calling to her softly. She ordered a cool cloth, which she pressed upon Merab's brow.

When Merab opened her eyes, Michal knew that she would not weep. She sat upon the bed and stared out through the window at a fluffy cloud scurrying by in the azure sky. When she spoke her voice was barely audible.

"Call the maid servants for me, Michal. I am in such disarray, and the noon hour approaches swiftly."

Michal clutched at Merab's hand, looking into her eyes intensely. "I could help you to escape, Merab. I know that Zerah would do anything for you. You and David could be wed in secret, where our father..."

"I am a princess, Michal, the daughter of Saul, the King of Israel." Merab stood to her feet and straightened to her full height, looking up into the eyes of her taller sister. "It is my duty to please my father, the king."

"But, Merab," Michal began.

Merab pulled her clutched hand away from Michal and lifted her chin gallantly. She looked at Michal with a depth of anguish in her liquid blue eyes. "One must do as one must do," she said. "Please call the maidservants."

CHAPTER 4

THE PRINCESS AND THE CAPTAIN

"For by thee I have run through a troop; and by my God have I leaped over a wall." Psalm 18:29

The astonished wedding guests attempted cheer, but dismay overcame some, and turning the wedding gowns back to the vestry, they departed to their homes. Merab sat silent and motionless, without expression upon her small, lovely face, throughout the days of the feast. Michal sought a chance to speak with Merab, but it avoided her. Never had she felt pain as she knew for her sister, yet she was helpless to aid. When the marriage feast at last closed, Merab went away with her husband, Adriel the Meholathite, accompanied by a host of handmaidens. No words could pass between them, but their eyes met in one swift, fleeting moment of boundless dialogue.

Michal reposed alone upon the broad terrace the day that David returned to the palace at Gibeah. When she saw him approach she hurried through the palace to the courtyard, Zerah upon her heels. Pushing past the servants who scurried forward to take the horses from the entering soldiers, Michal reached the horse of David first, grasping the bridle. David dismounted quickly and stood before Michal. His blue eyes asked the question before it rose to his lips. Michal did not hesitate, but spoke abruptly.

"My father has given the hand of Merab to Adriel the Meholathite in marriage."

David lowered his eyes and nodded his head slightly. "Yes," he told her, "I have received word."

Suddenly unable to speak, Michal gazed at the tall soldier before her. David had grown in stature and now wore a full beard. Yet, his face retained the boyish quality she had first noticed there, and his ready smile melted every expression into harmony.

He now smiled at her and said, "It was not the will of God that Merab should be my wife." He was confident as he said it, secure in his faith that God held the reins of his life in His hands.

Michal tried to return a smile, but remembered the bitter anguish of Merab's broken heart. David accepted it so blithely. Yet, Merab was now the wife of another. There was nothing that David could do.

Michal was suddenly struck with the thought; Merab was now the wife of another. She had only borne the burden of her sister's grief and dread of what David may do. She had not considered that with Merab's misfortune came her own possibility. David would not, could not wed her sister. Her heart burned within her breast until her cheeks flared, and she turned away quickly.

Merab's lamentable calamity faded from Michal's heart with her absence, until only a small corner of her soul harboured Merab's misfortune. The remainder of mind and soul were entangled in musings of David. The king received him privately, and then, curiously, David abode within the palace walls. No one spoke of the frustrated betrothal to Merab. David's smile and ready word still charmed the servants of the palace, men and women alike. And the beauty of his song once more enchanted each ear.

When the family royal gathered to hear David in concert once again, Michal's eyes were only for David. She cared not for the admiring glances of the sisters in law, nor the approving nod by the queen. Neither did she observe the dark cloud pass over her father's features as before. As the music rose upon the quiet evening air, there was no one but David. His heart poured forth from his lips in reverence to the Lord. He sang with his eyes closed for the most part, but once he looked intensely into Michal's gaze, and a gentle smile brushed his lips. She blessed the dimness of the room, for her face grew hot. She pressed her damp palms against her cheeks and breathed in the delicious sounds of David.

****

Attended closely by Zerah, Michal departed the palace walls astride an ambling donkey. She rode through the city gate and away down the gently declining mountain, across a rich meadow to a densely wooded glade, lush and green. There she dismounted and walked slowly, the donkey tugging at the rein to graze. She stooped to peer at ants running busily along a fallen tree limb, carrying parcels larger than they, intent upon their business. She leaned close to the forest floor to catch the inspiring beauty of a miniature wild flower. As she crouched thus, lost in the wonder before her, a single sweet strain caught upon the stillness and drifted to her. This sound was not familiar to her ear, and she led her mount toward its haunting melody. There, seated upon the stump of a felled tree, sat David. The mottled sunlight playing upon him through the leaves fairly concealed his face, but Michal recognized the frame of David. It was not a harp with which he made music, but a tiny wooden flute, perhaps carved by the musician himself. The song was light and joyful, as lambs cavorting about upon a field of green. For a moment Michal could imagine David sitting thus in a pasture of grass, surrounded by sheep which pressed against his knee to listen to his music, while their lambs danced about him.

When the song had done and faded, Michal knew that she could slip back the way she had come, unnoticed by the man before her. But she chose to make herself known. Pulling the donkey after her, she entered David's presence. He stood to his feet, and upon recognition, he knelt before her.

"Rise, David," Michal said.

David stood. He smiled a warm smile and waited for her to speak.

"What were you playing?" Michal asked him, gesturing

42

toward his instrument.

"This, My Princess, is a pipe. Did the music please you?"
Michal's scalp prickled at his words, "My Princess".

"Yes, it pleased me well. Will you play more?" she
asked.

With a sweeping nod David bowed and offered her the
seat upon the stump. Then, taking the reins from her hand, he
tied them securely to a sapling. He smiled into the shadows
between the trees and invited Zerah to approach and seat himself
as well. Zerah advanced, but remained standing, his arms folded
across his massive chest.

David lifted one leg to a fallen log and raised the pipe to
his lips. The sweet tones glided away from him to race about
among the branches of the trees and then float away toward the
hills. Michal sat enraptured, surrounded by the music, as by a
warm, comforting cloak, heedless of her hard seat, the damp
coolness of the air, or the passage of time.

When David had winded himself, he stretched his legs out
before him on the mossy forest floor at her side, leaning against
a tree trunk.

"Thank you," Michal whispered. "You play well."

David smiled his captivating smile at her and said, "I
spent many hours as a boy in the fields of my father with the
sheep. I had little to occupy my time, and therefore turned to
music for a companion."

"Who was your teacher?" Michal asked.

"The Lord was my teacher," David answered matter-of-
factly. "He has given me both the music and the words of my
songs." He gazed at her with his sapphire eyes and said softly,
"Even when I sing for others, for you, or for your father, my
song is to my God."

They sat in silence, listening to the whisper of the wood
about them, and Michal marvelled at the man who sat so close
beside her. "Can he hear the pounding of my heart?" she
wondered.

David suddenly stood to his feet, brushing the forest from his soldier's garb. He smiled at Michal through the dimness and said, "Come, My Princess, I shall escort you home. The supper hour draws near." He reached out a hand to her. Michal hesitated a moment, and then, placing her hand into his, allowed him to lift her from her thicket throne and lead her to her mount. David held the reins as they wound their way back to the palace, the princess astride the donkey, the captain walking at her side, the great black slave following closely.

Michal knew that she blushed at each glance from David, and tried to avoid looking toward him as they sat about the king's dinner table. Yet, she found her eyes upon him more than not. Jonathan engaged him in animated conversation, so she was spared the effort of speech. She chewed her food absently, intensely aware of David's presence, unable to control her thoughts enough to follow the conversation.

Michal pulled her eyes from David and saw her father watching her. She flushed a deeper crimson and lowered her eyes quickly. Her secret love for David need be concealed no longer, yet she knew her father's sentiments concerning his captain. Must her love for Saul prevent her love for David?

****

The family of the king shared the coolness of the wide veranda to break their fast. Servants scurried about bearing trays of flat breads and raisins, figs, dates, and pomegranates. Sweet nectars were poured from ornate jugs. Then the servants hurried away to await summons. Small children ran between reclining adults, playing games. The king lifted a fistful of dates to his mouth. Wiping his hand across his beard, he suddenly sat upright, searching the balcony with his eyes.

"Where is the son of Jesse?" he demanded. All eyes turned upon Saul, wondering. He rose to his feet and ordered a servant to fetch David.

David entered and bowed low before Saul. Saul munched another handful of fruit, chewing slowly. He kept his eyes upon the prostrate form before him as he drew a long drink from a goblet. Then he clapped his hands together quickly saying, "Rise, David!"

"David, I would have you to be my son in law," King Saul said slowly, rubbing his bearded chin. "My daughter Merab has been given in marriage to Adriel the Meholathite." Saul turned toward Michal and reached a hand to her. "Come here, Michal," he said. She approached warily, and took her father's hand. "David, I would have you take my daughter Michal to wife."[15] Saul took David's hand and placed Michal's into it.

Michal was abashed at her father's bluntness. All eyes were upon her, and upon David, of course. She dared not look at David's face, but she stood erect and raised her chin, ever so slightly, keeping her eyes upon her father. She let them lose their focus, so that she could more easily stare at him.

Saul smiled at them, then looked about the balcony, nodding and smiling. Turning back to the couple standing silent and still before him, he said, "Go, take a walk," and waved his fingers. David bowed toward the king and queen in turn and then led Michal away along the veranda. Zerah fell into step behind them.

Michal's fondest hope had just been promised her, yet her heart was uneasy as she and David strolled through the palace garden. Then David spoke. "I was once betrothed to your sister," he said. She knew that of course. Was he telling her that he preferred Merab? "Yet your father gave her to Adriel." David stopped walking and stood facing Michal. Emotions raged within her and she feared to look into his eyes lest they betray her, but his smile was gentle and easy, calming her. "Your father is changeable in his ways," he said softly. "Dare I hope, My

---

[15] I Samuel 18:21

Princess, that I may make you my wife? Or will my dreams be shattered by your father's changing moods?"

A flowering vine waved shining green leaves at her and bowed its bright blossoms in the breeze. Their scent filled her nostrils as her mind whirred wildly. David's words caressed her ears and kindled a new hope within her breast. He wished for her to be his wife! She smiled up at David through the tears which blurred her vision.

"I will hope, David," she said.

David looked into her eyes silently for a long moment. Then he flashed his carefree smile. "The Shepherd of my soul, and yours, Michal, shall guide our way. His way is right, whatever that may be."

Yes, Michal knew that David would follow his Shepherd without question, and accept the results as the will of God. Michal wished that she, too, could say, "The Shepherd of my soul will guide my way."

The servants of the palace were astir with excitement. Ziba had been commanded by King Saul, himself, to encourage the servants to speak with David and express to him the king's delight in him. The servants vied to be the first to encourage David to become the king's son in law. Zerah told Michal of the challenge from the king, and she pondered its reason. Did her father, indeed, delight in David? All the kingdom loved him, save the king, himself. Why should he desire so dearly that David marry Michal? Michal longed for Merab, to talk with her as always before. But Merab was not accessible, nor would she desire to discuss Michal's coming marriage to David.

Michal walked the palace gardens, accompanied by two of her maidens, who followed her, chatting and giggling about the young menservants of the palace. She blocked out their chatter, deep in contemplation of the pledge given by her father. She loved David. She wanted more than anything to be his wife. Yet, misgivings of her father's purpose prevented total elation at her betrothal to David. She rounded a tall green tree to find

David waiting for her. He took her hand and led her to a cushioned stone bench to sit.

"From many lips I have account that the king desires our union." He smiled at her and she smiled freely into his blue eyes.

"I am happy," she answered simply.

"But I am a poor man, Michal, unworthy to be the son in law of the King of Israel."

"You are a great hero in our nation!" Michal reprimanded him gently. "I only desire to be worthy to be your wife," she ended softly.

David smiled broadly, his eyes shining. "The servants of the palace have told me that the king requires no dowry save vengeance upon his enemies. He requires the tokens of the circumcision of one hundred Philistines for your hand, Michal."

"One hundred men must die that I may marry you?" Michal asked.

"They are the enemy. It is your father's desire. I leave with my men today," he told her. "When I return, I shall make you my wife."

Michal paced her chamber restlessly. She went to the window to peer into the darkness and then returned to her pacing. When she at last lay upon her bed, sleep would not come. Her heart feared for David. He had been gone but one day on his quest against the Philistines, but eternal hours they had been to Michal. A curious dread plagued Michal's heart. She knew that her father owned no love for David, although at one time he had greatly admired the shepherd musician. Why should he desire David to become his son in law unless it was in hopes that the Philistines would have the mastery over him in the battle? She tossed and turned upon her bed. Finally she arose and returned to the window. Peering into the moonless night, Michal tried to remember David's song, his favorite when singing to Saul:

The LORD is my shepherd; I shall not want.
He maketh me to lie down in green pastures:

He leadeth me beside the still waters.
He restoreth my soul:
He leadeth me in the paths of righteousness
*   for his name's sake.*
Yea, though I walk through the valley of the
shadow of death,
I will fear no evil:
For thou art with me; thy rod and thy staff
*   they comfort me.*[16]

Michal sang softly, the familiar tune helping her to remember the words. The valley of the shadow of death. "That is where David is," she thought. And surely David feared no evil. He knew that His Shepherd was with Him. He was comforted in the providence and love of the Lord.

She looked up into the sky and watched the distant stars winking in the blackness. "Oh, Lord God of David," she breathed. Never before had she attempted prayer away from the Tabernacle in Nob. "David trusts you fully. Please keep him from harm and bring him back safely and quickly." The sparkling stars continued their blinking in the inky sky. The familiar night droned on. Yet somehow Michal knew that the Great Deity sitting His throne in heaven had heard her simple petition.

When Michal awoke after a brief sleep, her heart no longer bore the dread of the night before. She patiently endured the maidens who dressed her, and took her morning meal upon the balcony, with a clear view of the road leading to the city. Zerah cast her an encouraging smile, aware of her nocturnal torment. She flashed a broad smile his way, then returned her gaze to the road.

She might wait thus for hours, or days perhaps, she knew. But she also knew that she would see David return, with the required fee for her father. In the early afternoon Michal saw a

---

[16] Psalm 23:1-4

file of horses following the road toward Gibeah. She ran to the battlement, clutching it in excitement. The horses bore riders. Yes! They were soldiers. David's men! And there at the lead, was David.

Michal descended the stairs swiftly and crossed the courtyard. She stood before the strong gates while Zerah opened them, and then she ran out along the road descending the mountainside. Stopping near the base of the mountain, she stood shading her eyes against the glaring sunlight. When David saw her, he urged his horse to a gallop. Pulling up so fiercely beside her that his horse reared to stop, David dismounted in one movement and clasped Michal's hands in his.

David's face was soiled, and his smile flashed white through his dusty beard. "The Lord blessed me in my campaign against the Philistines." He gestured toward two sacks tied to a horse behind him. "Here is the price of the dowry required by the king - doubled," David said happily. He looked back into Michal's eyes, elation lighting his blue ones. "Now you shall be my wife, Michal."

"I knew that the Lord would give you success, David. I prayed to Him for you," Michal told him. He tilted his head slightly to the side. Then, winking at her, he lifted her deftly onto his steed and climbed behind her. Together they rode up to the city.

The morning of her wedding to David was tremulous for Michal. The servants fluttered about her and her mother came to see to her toilet. Michal could only remember the morning of Merab's intended wedding to David, and she fearfully eyed the door. But the time elapsed and she descended the stairs and entered the glittering banquet room without interference from Saul. He greeted her, a taut smile on his lips, and led her to the table, where she sat, trembling, waiting for the groom to appear. David's wedding companions, he had told her, were to be his brothers and his sister's sons.

When the trumpets sounded and the great bronze doors

opened, Michal caught her breath. David, dressed simply in his captain's garb, entered with his fellows. His copper curls were cropped quite short, yet they coiled about his face and blended into his beard. His blue eyes shone. But it was his smile which lit the banquet hall. All eyes rested upon that smile and all hearts were warmed. All, Michal knew, but one. Saul reposed regally upon his couch, yet Michal detected a sulk upon his handsome face. But her eyes could look upon her father for only a moment, for the spectacle of David drew her gaze. And then David was at her side, bowing low before her. He did not rise from the bow, but settled upon one knee. Then she saw the small harp slung over his shoulder. He pulled it free, and plucking the strings softly, he sang a song of love to Michal. Her eyes stung and she let the tears slide along her nose and drip upon her wedding gown. Her nose began to run with emotion. She raised a laced kerchief to dab her nose and she smiled at David through misted eyes. He had told her that when he sang, he always sang to his God. But Michal knew, that now, this song was hers.

When David's love song had ended, sniffs echoed in the silent hall. David rose and took Michal's hand. He led her to the table where his mother and father sat, and seated her there. Then he looked about the immense room with a smile upon his magnificent face. He raised his arm in a waving salute to the guests, and a murmur surged through the room. Then David seated himself and the banquet was begun with joy.

The wedding feast of David and Michal continued a fortnight. The wedding guests, the residents of Gibeah, indeed all the subjects of Saul's kingdom rejoiced in the marriage of their champion to the daughter of the King. Abundant food and nectars, exhilarating entertainment, and incomparable music ruled the feast. The musician was David, himself, who sometimes mounted the rostrum to play and sing, and at other times meandered among the seated guests. Michal was amazed at his proficiency in producing music from various instruments. The wedding guests were enthralled by David's aptitude, and applauded his music fervently.

The wedding was such as Michal had never yet known, such as had never yet transpired in the palace of Gibeah. Yet, it was marriage that enraptured Michal. David's passion introduced her to new spheres. Together they discovered the miracle of becoming one flesh. She had been thoroughly enamoured of David before, but now he was her beloved, her husband. In the crowded banquet hall David and Michal could be alone in an adoring glance, a secret smile, a soft caress. In the privacy of the bridal chamber, they unlocked the doors to love's marvels.

Near the end of the first week of festivities, Jonathan reclined across the table from Michal. "To marry whom one must as well as whom one desires is pleasant, indeed," she told him with a smile. He lifted his goblet to her, smiling, then turned admiring eyes upon David.

On the Sabbath, Saul called David to the throne room for a conference and Michal waited, idly pacing the gardens, shadowed by Zerah. Merab found her there, and the two sat together in the deep shade of an oak. Merab, always slight of frame, looked thin and gaunt. She placed her hands upon her abdomen and turned large, pathetic eyes to Michal.

"I am the wife of Adriel. Here," she said, "I carry his child. But here," Merab placed her hands over her heart, "I carry David. He is your husband, I know. But I love him." She turned her eyes away from Michal's gaze. "I shall always love David."

CHAPTER 5

THE PRINCESS AND THE OUTLAW

"Yea, mine own familiar friend, in whom I trusted, which did eat of my bread, hath lifted up his heel against me." Psalm 41:9

David sought to personally bid farewell to each wedding guest, with Michal at his side. The visitors departed with cheerful hearts, some singing to themselves the songs of David. Saul presented Michal with ten maidservants and David with a grand house across the city from the palace. Michal asked that she might also have Zerah, her faithful guardian, and was granted her desire.

David bounded up and down the staircase of their house. He darted from one lavish room to the next, skipping like one of his lambs, exclaiming to Michal about the grandeur of each. Together they stood upon their balcony and viewed the panorama of blue sky and green earth. David's enthusiasm over every detail of their new life fired Michal's heart with joy. Her face ached from smiling with David, and her happiness filled her to overflowing. She wondered if love were so wondrous to every newly wedded man and his wife. Yet, she knew that it was not, for she was aware of Merab's despair. And she knew that in all the world there was not another like David.

Michal and David lay in their bed, breaking their fast upon fish and cucumbers, bread and fruit. Zerah knocked and was beckoned by David. He bowed low before his master and mistress. "The General Abner wishes to speak with you," he said.

Michal sat up against the bedstead. "He is my uncle, David," she said. "You may see him here."

Abner entered and bowed slightly. Michal greeted him brightly, but he barely acknowledged her greeting and turned to David. "The princes of the Philistines have passed into Judah once more," he said. "Saul has ordered your troops to meet them."

David sighed and looked at Michal. Then he turned to Abner. "Very well. Thank you, Abner."

When Abner had gone, Michal clung to David. "Why must you go?" My father has many soldiers to fight against the Philistines."

"He knows that the soldiers of my command will defeat them," David said. But Michal feared other purpose in her father's orders.

When David had gone with his soldiers to meet the Philistines, Michal wandered through her large house aimlessly. She was married to a soldier, and she must learn to pass the hours, the days, when he must leave to wage battle against the enemy. Michal knew that the Philistines hated David particularly because he had slain Goliath. Yet, she also knew that the hand of the Lord was upon David.

With a canopy of stars above her Michal sat in her courtyard, Zerah never far from her. Once again she attempted prayer. "Oh Lord of David," she began. "He trusts You so implicitly. Please protect him from his enemies." She hesitated. "Even though my father's design may be for his harm, keep him safe, oh God in Whom he puts his trust."

In the bright sunlight, shaded by a shield which Zerah held above her, Michal laid her stitchery down and prayed for David. At her waking, when she lay down to sleep, and ever in between, Michal prayed to David's God for his protection.

Michal was borne upon a litter for most of her evening meals to the palace to sup with her parents. It was there that details of the battle were discussed. Great glowing reports of the cunning strategy of David were delivered by envoys from the battlefield. He was reported to be the wisest of Saul's officers in the battle against the Philistines.[17] In a flurry bordering rage, Saul left for the battlefield with a company of men.

The armies of Israel marched home again with great fanfare. The terrible enemy was not beaten, but was put at bay for the moment, and the soldiers returned home. Michal met her husband on the hill where once before she had awaited his return, and he embraced her fondly. Then, lifting her to his steed as before, they rode together to the palace.

Michal made no notice of her father's mood nor Jonathan's strained expression. David was his usual light-hearted self, and her eyes could not leave his face; her ears heard only his voice. She was happy. Her husband had returned and she was near him. His presence filled her with a warm content.

As David fetched the litter to carry Michal home, Jonathan caught her elbow and pulled her behind a broad pillar. "Be watchful," Jonathan said. Michal knit her brow, uncertain what he meant. He continued. "When our father came to the battle he spoke with me and also with all of his servants and ordered David's death."

Michal caught her breath and whispered, "David?"

"I warned David to hide secretly until I had spoken with our father. I pleaded with Father for David." Jonathan looked intently into Michal's eyes. She knew his next words were spoken to convince himself as well as her. "Father promised in the name of the Lord that David would not be slain."[18] He hesitated. "But be watchful. Just be watchful."

David did not mention Saul's murderous intent to Michal. He took Michal to their home and they resumed the rapturous life to which they had been introduced for so short a time. David tried to fit the role of wealthy householder, but his heart turned often to the simple beauties of his rearing. Hours passed in

---

[17] I Samuel 18:30

[18] I Samuel 19:6

conversation with the servants, and he often carried parcels up and down the stairs for the maidservants. All of David's menservants and maidservants loved him, Michal knew. She smiled to see Zerah and David in spirited conversation. "Two of the men whom I love the most," she thought to herself, and then was startled at the revelation. Yes, she loved Zerah. Not as she loved David, nor as she loved her father or Jonathan. But yes, she trusted and adored the strong black slave.

Wearied by the life of luxury into which he was pressed, David wakened Michal one bright morning with a proposal. "Let's take a journey to visit my family," he said. Michal noted his longing in the words, and preparations were begun at once.

When Michal descended to the courtyard for the journey, she found David smiling broadly at the reins of an iron chariot taken in battle from the Philistines. Settling her upon a seat which he had positioned beside him, David coaxed the horses into motion. Several of David's soldiers, five maidservants, Zerah, and a cart containing Michal's necessities, made up the caravan toward Bethlehem.

Bethlehem was a small city, nestled upon the top of a rocky hill and surrounded by a tall stone wall. As they neared the city, greetings came from each one they met. A small boy ran ahead of them, shouting the news that the great hero of Israel had returned to the city of his boyhood. Michal rose and stood at David's side in the chariot. Throngs lined the road through the gate of the city. Flowers were plucked and thrown into the chariot and upon the road before them. Michal gathered a bouquet from the chariot and pressed them to her nose. David waved to the people of Bethlehem. As they entered the gate of the city, David drew the horses to a halt. He jumped from the chariot and lifted Michal to the ground. Then, taking her hand, he led her to where his ancient father and short, round mother waited expectantly beside the well of Bethlehem. David embraced and kissed them both. Michal had only met them at the marriage feast, but she followed David's example, smiling at these people who were now her family.

Michal also greeted each of David's brothers and sisters with their spouses and children. To the great delight of David's small nephews and nieces, he held each aloft in turn, laughing with them and twirling them through the air. Never had Michal heard so much laughter. Never had she experienced such warmth and closeness as David's family demonstrated.

When they reached the two story stone house of Jesse and his wife, the whole assemblage entered, filling the room from wall to wall. David's men were led by a boy to the stables. David and Michal were seated on a long bench at a table in the center of the room, and David's sisters in law bathed the feet of David and Michal. The adults seated themselves, crowding close to catch each word of David. Michal's handmaidens were also awkwardly seated. Zerah stood against the wall, arms folded, face set. The children ran about the room, or pressed close to David, stroking his beard, fingering his garments, smiling into his face, or openly staring at Michal. He lifted one small girl to his lap. Turning toward Michal he said, "Ruth, this is my beautiful bride. Isn't she lovely?"

"She's a princess," the little girl answered.

"Yes, she is," David said, winking at Michal. "Ruth is named for a great grandmother of mine who lived here in this very house," David told Michal. Then he kissed his little niece on the cheek and set her down.

David's mother bustled about, happy tears coursing down her face. She set a large, steaming bowl of food on the table and a plate of flat bread. Suddenly everyone hushed. "David," Jesse said. "Will you thank the Lord for this food?"

David raised his eyes to heaven and spoke. His words were a song without music. Even the little ones were quiet, listening to the praise and thanks offered to God. Sitting there, hearing his prayer, Michal knew that God was listening, too.

When David was done, everyone tore a piece from the loaf of bread and each dipped it into the steaming bowl, lifting the thick gravy to their lips. As the loaf melted away, it was instantly replaced with another. The food was spicy and warm, with chunks of meat and vegetables. The bread was soft and delicious. Altogether the meal was excellent, although Michal had never known such food as this. David lifted his cup and smiled at Michal. "There is no water in Israel like the water from the well of Bethlehem." His comment was loudly lauded around the table, and everyone joined David in drinking the remarkable water.

When the meal had ended, Michal saw David's sisters and sisters in law rise from the table and carry the dishes away. One brought a damp cloth and washed the smooth, shining surface of the table. While the men sat about the table talking, Michal watched the women of the family wash the dishes that had been used for the meal and the cooking vessels. Michal spoke to her handmaids and they attempted to take over the job of cleaning, but David's mother shooed them back to the table. There seemed to be no servants present at all. Yet, the women who chatted together as they worked at the end of the very room in which they had dined, did not seem discontent with the task.

David's mother came to the table and seated herself beside Michal. Only then did Michal realize that she had not sat with them for the meal. Perhaps she herself had eaten while serving her family.

Her mother in law smiled at her and took her hands in her own plump ones. "We are so happy for David. We know that he is very happy to have you as his wife. And we welcome you into our family, Michal." She pronounced Michal's name with a pleasant twist which she had never before heard. Instantly Michal liked the woman before her.

"I am happy to be a part of your family," Michal told her. She turned her eyes to David, who was intently conversing with the men. "I am very happy to be David's wife."

The maidservants, much to their dismay, were sent to the homes of David's brothers to sleep, but they appeared early each morning to care for Michal's toilet. Michal noticed that the women of David's family tended to their own grooming, or asked help of each other.

The days spent with David's family were novel and exciting for Michal. She learned that there were no servants, but that the families worked together to accomplish the work. Together the men, when not accompanying the army of Saul, were superintended by their father to farm the fields, dress the vines, and keep the olive and date trees. The boys of the family were the shepherds, and David seemed to have a special esteem for them. Together the women ground the grain into flour and baked the daily bread. Together they carded wool and spun the rough flax into linen. They wove their own cloth and fashioned from it the clothing for their husbands and children, as well as their own dress. They washed the clothing, beating them hard against large rocks to loosen the soil, and hung them out to dry. They trimmed the lamps and stoked the fires. They cooked and cleaned. They fed and dressed and bathed their children, someone having always an infant clutched to her breast, as together they laboured. Michal's maidservants sat idly about uncomfortably, until they were at last allowed to assist with the daily tasks.

David went often with the men to their responsibilities, and Michal watched the women work in harmony, savoring the experience. She tried her hand at baking bread, first grinding the grain into fine flour, and was pleased with her success. She rolled back the sleeves of her costly garments and scrubbed the clothing of a sister in law's small children. She made a savoury stew, herself, and when David was told at mealtime, he rose from his seat, and grabbing Michal, twirled her around in his strong embrace. "It's wonderful!" he exulted over her cooking. She blushed deeply, aware that all eyes were upon her, yet caring only for the loving gaze of David.

Every evening, when the toil of the day had ended, the family sat together to listen to David. Michal watched the faces of these people who loved her husband, and saw there a devotion and satisfaction which she, the daughter of King Saul, envied. They loved David, not because he was a hero or that he had married the daughter of the king, but for himself. And they loved each other equally as well. She knew this as she sat with them, watching the shadows from the evening fire play upon their faces, hearing the beautiful music of David. That music which was lovely above all other, was somehow lovelier here in this humble home with these simple people.

David took Michal to the shepherd's fields to see the very place where he, as a lad, had watched the sheep of his father. There David fashioned a small flute and taught a nephew to produce music on the lonely hillside. Michal rubbed the heads of lambs and sheep. They crushed against her skirts, soiling her rich gown, stamping upon her feet, but she did not mind. She was sharing with David the place and people dearest to his heart.

They mounted a stone covered hill where two caves entered the rock and sat upon two large stones positioned inside the mouth of one cave. From this vantage point Michal surveyed the hills and fields, woods and streams so cherished by David.

Zerah accompanied them upon each hike, staying far back, but near enough to see to Michal's security. David invited him to join them, but he merely nodded and kept a discrete distance.

As they sat atop the shepherds' hill one late afternoon, the shadows painting stripes across the fields, David took Michal's hand. She looked into his eyes and saw there a strange sadness. He smiled faintly. His voice was soft when he spoke.

"The Lord has chosen me, My Princess, to someday be the King of His people, Israel."

Michal did not understand his statement at once. Then comprehension dawned. "Jonathan is heir to the throne of Israel," she told him. "And his son after him."

David pursed his lips, then licked them and continued. "When I was a youth, before I came to Gibeah to play before your father, the prophet Samuel came to Bethlehem. The Lord chose me as king, and Samuel there anointed me. At God's appointed time I shall be king."[19]

Michal frowned. "But Jonathan..."

"I love Jonathan as a brother, more than a brother. I would give my life for him. I will not dispossess him of his throne. But at God's appointed time I shall be king."

David's curious words hung in Michal's heart long after they climbed the hill to Bethlehem.

When the visit had ended and they prepared to return to Gibeah, Michal was sorry, indeed. Here at last she had experienced the way of life of the common Israelite. Here she had also discovered a comradeship foreign to the life of the palace of Saul. She embraced her mother in law, now a dear friend to her, with tears stinging her eyes.

"Do come again, soon," her mother in law invited. "We always love to see David, and we all love you, too, Michal."

Michal's heart sang. Her family loved one another, but it was not a subject of conversation. She smiled into her mother in law's face. "I hope we shall come again, soon. I have enjoyed my visit greatly."

Soon after Michal's return to Gibeah, Merab came to the palace to await the birth of her child. Saul paid small mind to the matter, for Merab's children were inconsequential to the throne of Israel. Merab's soldier husband was not there when his first born son came. On the eighth day he was circumcised[20] and named Joel.

David was home far too short a time before he was summoned to King Saul, and commissioned to lead his troops to meet the Philistines, who once again marched against God's people. The daily messengers brought tidings of the great

---

[19] I Samuel 16:1-13

[20] Genesis 17:10

slaughter of the enemy by David and his men. The Philistines
could not resist the troops of David, and fled from him.²¹ The
victorious army returned home, with great jubilation. Yet, as
before, the multitudes of Israel lauded David, now their well
beloved hero. Saul did not attempt to conceal his resentment.
He strode away from the welcoming crowds, directly to his
throne room to sulk.

Nob had ever been a place of relish for Michal, but as she
and David stood together before the Tabernacle of the Lord to
offer the sacrifices of the Lord, new wonder was born. The
duties performed at the altar of the Lord had always been to her
a necessary part of life, but hardly more.

David carried the lamb for their sacrifice in his arms to
the door of the Tabernacle. It kicked against the fine fabric of his
garment and bleated loudly. With great gentleness David set the
lamb upon the ground, caressing its head and back with tender
strokes. "He is a shepherd still," Michal mused silently. David
took the sharp knife proffered by the priest. Holding the lamb
with his left hand, he held forth the knife, the long slender blade
glinting in the sunlight.

"This lamb must die, Michal, because of our iniquities."
Michal saw a tear slide along David's nose.

"Do you sorrow for the lamb?" she asked gently.

"I sorrow that I am a sinner and my sin displeases my
Lord."

David bowed his head in silent prayer. Then, with one
swift motion, the throat of the lamb was slit. The priest stooped
and caught the blood in a small basin. He then sprinkled the
blood of the lamb upon the altar and all around the sides of it.
The carcass of the lamb was then placed upon the altar and
burned unto the Lord.²²

---

²¹ I Samuel 19:8

²² Leviticus 3:1-5

David walked Michal to the door of Jehoaddan's house and kissed her lightly. "I will return soon." He smiled and turned to stride away toward the home of his friend, Abiathar, a son of Ahimelech the priest.

As always the princess and the daughter of the priest, now the wife of a priest as well, found sweet fellowship in one another's company. Michal had not visited her friend since her marriage to David, and the two now shared a new dimension of perception. They talked and laughed together, each joying in the happiness of the other, secure and warm in each other's love, until David came to fetch away his bride.

Returned home, David and Michal had gone to their bed when a knock came at their door. Zerah announced a call from the palace to soothe the king's tormented spirit. David kissed Michal and bearing his small harp left with the servants of Saul.

Michal paced the room, then exited to the balcony and reclined beneath the night sky. She breathed in the cool night air and watched the constellations twinkle in their courses through the sky. She hoped only that her father could be quickly pacified and David could come home.

A tumult below sent Michal down to the outer door where she met David. His sapphire eyes were wide as he ordered the door latched and guarded. Taking Michal's elbow he propelled her to an inner room. There he embraced her, resting his cheek against her forehead. She felt him tremble. "David?" she whispered.

David looked down at Michal. A crystal drop fell from his beard and plummeted to the floor. Then she saw that his eyes were moist and his beard was wet. Wet with tears. She waited. David swallowed hard and then spoke, a choke almost stealing his voice.

"As I sang, the king once more thrust a javelin at me."[23]

---

[23] I Samuel 20:9

His arms around her tightened and she felt his body quiver. "I love your father, Michal. Why does he want to kill me? What have I done to offend him?"

Michal had no answer for David. The spirit of evil which enshrouded her father's soul was past understanding.

They returned to their bedroom, and a heavy guard was placed beside the door. David and Michal clung desperately to each other in the somber silence. Dread began in Michal's heart and slowly crept throughout her being as she stood in David's intense embrace. Would their life ever be lived in fear of her father's wrath against David? Perhaps they should go to another city of Israel to live. She thought fondly of Bethlehem. No, even there Saul would find David, if his intent were murder.

David released his embrace and reached for his small harp. Kneeling upon the floor, facing toward the tall, open window, David composed a song of pain and sorrow, trust and hope in God.

"Deliver me from mine enemies, O my God:
Defend me from them that rise up against me.
Deliver me from the workers of iniquity,
And save me from bloody men.
For, lo, they lie in wait for my soul:
The mighty are gathered against me;
Not for my transgression, nor for my sin, O LORD.
They run and prepare themselves without my fault:
Awake to help me, and behold.
Thou therefore, O LORD God of hosts,
The God of Israel,
Awake to visit all the heathen:
Be not merciful to any wicked transgressors.
They return at evening:
They make a noise like a dog, and go round about the
city.
Behold, they belch out with their mouth:
Swords are in their lips:

For who, say they, doth hear?
But thou, O LORD, shalt laugh at them;
Thou shalt have all the heathen in derision.
Because of his strength will I wait upon thee:
For God is my defence.
The God of my mercy shall prevent me:
God shall let me see my desire upon mine enemies.
Slay them not, lest my people forget:
Scatter them by thy power;
And bring them down, O Lord our shield.
For the sin of their mouth and the words of their lips
Let them even be taken in their pride:
And for cursing and lying which they speak.
Consume them in wrath, consume them,
That they may not be:
And let them know that God ruleth in Jacob
Unto the ends of the earth.
And at evening let them return;
And let them make a noise like a dog,
And go round about the city.
Let them wander up and down for meat,
And grudge if they be not satisfied.
But I will sing of thy power;
Yea, I will sing aloud of thy mercy in the morning:
For thou hast been my defence and refuge in the day
        of my trouble.
Unto thee, O my strength, will I sing:
For God is my defence, and the God of my mercy."[24]

David lunged to his feet at a sudden knock on the door.
He went to the door and there found Zerah. "Master," Zerah
said in great agitation. "There are men lurking outside, watching
the house. They are men of His Majesty, King Saul."

---

[24] Psalm 59

"Set men to watch them, Zerah," David told him. Then, thanking the tall black slave, David closed the bedroom door.

Michal was instantly at David's side. She grasped his arm, squeezing hard. "David, Father has sent them here to watch until the morning and kill you when you leave the house!"

"Why, Michal?" David asked, agony drenching his voice. "Why does he seek my hurt?"

Michal buried her face against his chest, and he held her tightly. Together they wept.

"You must leave," Michal told David suddenly. "Tonight. Now!"

David held Michal and looked sadly into her eyes. "Yes," he said. "I must flee from the king's wrath." David kissed Michal tenderly, their tears mingling.

David beckoned Zerah and asked the positions of the prowling soldiers. "This window is the safest place to descend," David told Michal. "There are no guards below because of the wall and no exits."

"But how?" Michal asked.

David smiled through his tears. "My great grandmother let two spies down through a window by a rope."[25] Then, turning to Zerah, he ordered a thick rope, which David tied tightly to the bedstead. Zerah brought a small bundle of bread and cheese as well. Then he left the room, closing the door.

"Michal," David said, embracing his wife. "I must escape from your father. I love you. I will pray that I may soon return to you." He gave her a final kiss and turned to the rope. "Pull this up as soon as I have descended." David slid down swiftly. He turned and raised a hand in salute. Then he was gone into the night.

---

[25] Joshua 2:15

CHAPTER 6

THE PRINCESS AND THE FUGITIVE

"Deliver me, O LORD, from mine enemies: I flee unto thee to hide me." Psalm 143:9

Michal paced the room anxiously. She often paused to peer out the window into the darkness where David had vanished. A sliver of moon had risen above the trees, kissing the blackness with a soft silver hue. She wrung her hands desperately, her spirit groaning in helplessness. Suddenly she stopped. "Zerah," she ordered, "Fetch to me an image the size of David."

Zerah brought from the courtyard a statue of stone, a vestige of the rebellious days when judges ruled the land.[26] With muscles bulging and a fine sweat breaking out across his brow the large black man hefted the image onto the bed at Michal's direction. She put a pillow of goat's hair upon the bolster and pulled a blanket up snugly to appear as a man asleep in bed.

As the dawn broke, messengers from Saul knocked on the door of David's house. The attendants of the house escorted the envoys to the bedroom. With Zerah standing close behind her, Michal answered the knock upon the bedroom door.

"King Saul has bidden David immediately," a messenger told her.

Michal gestured toward the bed. "David is ill," she told the man. "Please give my father David's regrets. He will report as soon as he is well."

As Michal watched the entourage file from the house Zerah spoke. "They will return, Princess. Your father will not yield so easily."

---

[26] Judges 2:17

"Yes, Zerah," Michal said. "I know that is true." She walked to the window and watched the morning maturing before her. The creatures of the night of David's escape had gone to their resting places and those of the day now awoke and stirred. Soft pink light caressed the stones of the city wall, transforming into a radiant golden glow as the sun climbed into the sky. Michal watched the wall and the forest below, pondering her husband's escape.

"David," she breathed. "David, where are you? What are you doing?" Michal did not know where David was. But she knew what he was doing. He was praying to his God. He was trusting in his God. He was following the hand of his God as He led David away from Gibeah, away from Michal.

"Oh Lord of David," Michal prayed. "If ever David has needed your protection, he needs it now." She stopped to contemplate, and then continued. "You have delivered him from the hand of the giant Goliath, and from the troops of the Philistines again and again. Oh, God," she cried, the tears spilling over, "protect David from my father!"

The dreaded knock came soon. The servants were sluggish in answering, and the envoys annoyed and angry. They barged through the doorway and bolted up the stairs with the servants in pursuit, scolding. They did not knock upon the bedroom door, but opened it. Zerah stood before them, arms folded across the massive chest, face set as stone.

"Out of the way, slave!" ordered the captain. Then, addressing Michal, the man said, "Saul has ordered for David to be brought to him in the bed." The soldiers pushed past Zerah. The captain, reaching the bed first, threw back the blanket. Silence fell suddenly upon the soldiers as they saw the image in the bed.

"Search the house!" the captain ordered. The soldiers scattered, tearing doors open, peering into corners and nooks. Satisfied that David was not to be found in the house, they returned to the captain. Irritated by his failure to procure David, he turned again toward Michal. "Take her to the king," he ordered.

The soldiers grasped Michal's arms to escort her forth, but Zerah stepped between the men and the girl, and they loosed their grip. "The princess is able to convey herself to the king," the black man intoned. The soldiers stepped back and allowed Michal to proceed alone, escorted by Zerah.

As the captain preceded Michal into the throne room Saul rose from his seat. "Where is David?" he demanded.

"He was not there, Your Highness," answered the captain. "We searched the house. In the bed was an image made to appear like a man sleeping."

Saul turned his eyes, hot with rage, upon Michal. She watched the anger melt away into a deep sadness. He approached her, taking her hands in his. "Why have you deceived me, Michal? Why have you sent my enemy away and helped him escape?"

The pain on Saul's visage caused Michal to turn her eyes away from him. "He threatened to kill me," Michal lied to him. "He forced me to help him escape."[27]

Saul did not let her hands go. He stood still, staring at his daughter as the court looked on. Michal felt the stares upon her, but she held her head high. The tears stung the backs of her eyes, but not one slid free. The sobs were held at bay only by her determination. She swallowed and lifted her chin yet higher.

"So be it," Saul said at last, releasing her hands. He stretched himself to his full, imposing height, and spoke to Abner. "Take a troop and find him."

Michal's mother suggested that she stay at the palace, but Michal declined. She must remain at home, for it was there that David would return. The servants were kind, gentle, smiling with compassionate understanding. The master they loved was a

---

[27] I Samuel 19:17

fugitive from the king. The father of the princess sought her husband's life.

Michal secluded herself in her house. Although her handmaids were always near, and the house was filled with servants, it was Zerah with whom she found comfort. The black slave was never far from her side, he would listen to her attentively, and his words were wise and comforting. But her heart ached for David.

Michal had heard nothing for several days, when Jonathan came to speak with her. She led him to a cool, airy room, and together they sipped nectar. Servants fanned them against the heat.

"Do you know where David is?" Michal asked.

Jonathan nodded slowly. "We received word that he was with Samuel in Naioth. Father sent messengers to take David, but when they arrived in Naioth and witnessed Samuel and the company of the prophets prophesying, they prophesied also! Two more times our father sent messengers and the same thing happened. At last our father himself went." Jonathan looked sadly at Michal. "Father's malice toward David is great. But the Lord God is greater, little sister. When Father arrived in Naioth he, also, prophesied. He completely lost control of himself all day and all night.[28] David was afforded a chance of escape."

"In Naioth," Michal repeated. "Oh, Jonathan, please find David. Tell him of my love for him and how I miss him." She looked pleadingly into her brother's eyes. "How much I need him," she said.

Jonathan took her hand and squeezed it gently. "I spoke with David after he fled from Naioth. I will see him again, soon, Michal."

"You spoke with him? O, Jonathan, I must see him! When will you see him again?"

---

[28] I Samuel 19:24

Jonathan placed two fingers across his sister's lips. "Silence, little sister. David's life depends upon secrecy."

Ahinoam, the wife of Saul, came to her daughter's home to request her presence for the feast of the new moon. "You are expected to be there, my dear," the queen said.

Michal looked away from her mother's gaze. "The king attempted to kill my husband," she said softly.

Silence held all sound as the moments passed. Ahinoam began to speak, then hesitated. She seemed to search the ceiling for the words to say. Her voice was uncertain when she said, "Your husband is expected at the feast as well."

Michal's eyes darted to her mother's face. She rose to her feet as she said, "David?" Falling to her knees beside her mother's couch she asked, "Will David be at the feast, Mother?"

Ahinoam looked away from the pleading gaze and, this time repeated strongly, "Your husband is expected at the feast."

Michal studied her mother's face for a moment. "Yes, Mother," she said. "I will attend the feast."

With the commencement of the feast of the new moon, Michal was decked in rich apparel and she went to the dining hall of the king. Her brothers and their wives sat at the table. Ahinoam sat along the wall on the right side of Saul with Abner on his left. But David's seat, at Michal's side, was empty. Michal could not choke down the meal, however fine the fare. She avoided the glowering eyes of Saul. Her eyes pled with Jonathan's for an explanation, yet she received none.

In great disappointment and emptiness Michal returned to her house. David had not come to the feast. She lay across her bed and wept in loneliness, great sobs shaking her body until exhaustion carried her into the sweet escape of sleep.

Michal hesitated to prepare for the feast the second night of the new moon. A strange tension now existed between herself and her parents, and much effort was necessary on the parts of all to preserve a sense of normalcy. Yet, what if David were to indeed appear at the feast as was expected? Michal shook off her reserve and went to the festivities.

To her great melancholy, yet not surprise, David was once more absent from the feast. Saul shifted in his seat with agitation. He did not address Michal, knowing full well her ignorance as to David's whereabouts. But, leaning over the table to look Jonathan squarely in the eye, Saul asked him, "Why does the son of Jesse not attend the feast of the new moon, neither yesterday nor today?"

"David earnestly asked leave of me to go to Bethlehem," Jonathan said. His fair face reddened as he explained. "He asked to go to a family sacrifice in the city. He said that his brother had commanded him to be there, and if he had found favour in my eyes, that I might let him go and see his brothers. That is why he has not come to the king's table."

Michal's heart burned within her. Oh, how she wished to be with David in Bethlehem! "I will go with a train to Bethlehem in the morning," she planned silently. "I will go to David, since he has not come to me."

Michal was wrenched from her musings by the crashing of her father's couch as it toppled sideways. He stood, towering above the table, glaring at Jonathan.

"You son of a perverse, rebellious woman!" Saul shouted. "I know that you have chosen the son of Jesse to your own confusion." Saul paused. Then his voice softened, touched with compassion, "For as long as the son of Jesse lives, you will not be established as King of Israel. Send and fetch him to me, Jonathan, and he will surely die."

"Why should David be killed, Father? What has he done?"

Instantly livid with rage, Saul grasped a javelin from the corner and flung it at Jonathan, lightly grazing his right shoulder. Jonathan rose from his seat, anger coloring his face crimson. Taking Neziah's hand, he led her from the room, leaving their dinners untouched.

Saul watched his son leave. Then he turned his eyes to

survey the dismayed faces before him. "Eat!" he commanded. "This is the feast of the new moon. Eat!" He righted his couch and seated himself once again. Lifting a leg of lamb, he began to chew with zeal.

The sun had climbed into the sky but a little distance, when Michal, with a train of servants and the faithful Zerah, began her journey toward Bethlehem; toward David. A solitary figure was wending its way along the road toward the city, and as they neared, Michal recognized Jonathan. He waved his arm and ran toward her.

"Where are you going?" he asked. In alarm, Michal saw that his eyes were red and swollen, and his beard wet with tears.

"I go to Bethlehem to be with David," she told him.

Jonathan shook his head. "David is not in Bethlehem. I just now have come from meeting him in yonder field. I have told him that the king indeed desires his death, and he has gone."

"David was here? Where has he gone?" Michal asked.

"He has fled from our father"s wrath," Jonathan answered sadly.

"But where?"

"Where he can hide in safety," Jonathan said, climbing up beside Michal. "Turn the wagons and return to the city."[29]

When the feast of the new moon had passed, Michal secluded herself once again at her home. She cast her eyes often out the window through which David had departed. The city was closely guarded, and Michal's house was watched. She knew that David would have great difficulty entering the city to deliver her and take her away with him. Yet, she knew that he would. He must.

Michal was summoned to the king. She stood before her father, her heart aching with love for him, yet breaking because of his hatred for her husband.

---

[29] I Samuel 20:27-42

"Come," Saul said, extending his hand toward her. Michal mounted the steps to stand before his throne. The king studied her face for a moment and then spoke. "It is not good for you to be alone in a big house. I have given the house to another and you will come back to the palace."

Michal's countenance held, but her heart leapt within her breast. "It is David's house, Father. You gave it to David." Her voice wavered only the slightest.

"David is no longer here. I doubt that he will have further use for the house."

The servants in attendance stared straight ahead, yet they strained to hear. David was their beloved musician. Michal was David's wife. They knew that the heart of the king would stop at nothing upon which it was set.

"Father," Michal said, her voice barely audible as she endeavored control. "David is my husband. He will return and we will live together at the house."

Saul raised one eyebrow. "I have given the house to another."

Great restraint was necessary to see Michal through the move from David's house back to the palace. With face set and walking upright and rigid, Michal refused the litter and wended her way through the streets of Gibeah to her parents' home. Zerah carried upon his back the small chest into which Michal had put every vestige of David. It held the small harp, shepherds' garb, and a small, leather sling.

Michal settled into the rooms which she and Merab had shared. She lived as a widow in the house of her father. She ate at her father's table, but she would not speak. However, when Jonathan supped with them, she always sought news of David from him.

Every night Michal slept lightly, with her window open, hoping that each would be the night when David would come and take her away with him.

With little to occupy her interest and time, Michal

descended one day to the archives where the chronicles of the king's business were kept. There, labelled and wrapped in soft cloth coverings, were the scribes' carefully penned narratives of battles, relations with neighboring kingdom's, details of trade, and accounts of palace life. Coughing from the shifted dust, Michal came upon an old scroll wrapped in scarlet . She shook the dust away and slipped the parchment from its case. Written in a tight, yet stilted cipher, unlike any she had seen by the hand of the scribes, was a copy of the law of Moses.

Michal carried the large scroll from its niche to a slit in the wall through which bright sunshine was emitted. She was familiar with much of the law, and had been tutored in the stories of Scripture as a child. Yet, it was with awe that she read the sacred words for herself, of the creation of the universe, of Adam and Eve's iniquity, of the promise of a Savior.[30]

A shadow fell across the words and she looked up to find the old scribe Zelophehad watching her.

"Does the Princess savor the holy Scriptures?" he asked.

"Yes," she answered simply.

"The scroll which you have chosen was penned by King Saul many years ago, and has not been disturbed until now."

"My father penned this scroll?" Michal asked incredulously.

"Your Majesty," answered the old man, "God commanded to Moses, long before your father's day, that when Israel chose a king he was to copy out for himself a copy of the law of Moses."[31]

Michal looked through new eyes at the manuscript before her. Her father, so at enmity with God and man, had once carefully written each word of God here. "Might I take this copy with me to my rooms to better read it?" she asked.

---

[30] Genesis chapters 1-3

[31] Deuteronomy 17:18

The old scribe nodded, and helped her replace the scarlet cover.

Secluded in her rooms, Michal read the Scriptures, given by God to Moses. From a child she had been schooled in the Scriptures and taught about God. But now, reading each word for herself, she learned to know God. He was a God of wrath, destroying those who hated Him. And yet, He was a God of love and gentle care for those who trusted Him. David must surely have read the law of God to know Him so intimately and love Him so dearly. When Michal had completed the first book of Moses, she prayed in simplicity and sincerity to the Author of those words. "Oh, Lord of David, I wish for You to be my Lord as well. I wish to know and love You as David knows and loves You. I wish to trust you, Lord, as David does."

When Michal read the last book of Moses she came upon the words of the Lord which Zelophehad had mentioned the day she had discovered her father's scroll.

"When thou art come unto the land which the LORD thy God giveth thee, and shalt possess it, and shalt dwell therein, and shalt say, I will set a king over me, like as all the nations that are about me; Thou shalt in any wise set him king over thee, whom the LORD thy God shall choose: one from among thy brethren shalt thou set king over thee: thou mayest not set a stranger over thee, which is not thy brother. But he shall not multiply horses to himself, nor cause the people to return to Egypt, to the end that he should multiply horses: forasmuch as the LORD hath said unto you, Ye shall henceforth return no more that way. Neither shall he multiply wives to himself, that his heart turn not away: neither shall he greatly multiply to himself silver and gold. And it shall be, when he sitteth upon the throne of his kingdom, that he shall write him a copy of this law in a book out of that which is before the priests the Levites: And it shall be with him, and he shall read therein all the days of his life: that he may learn to fear the LORD his God, to keep all the words of this law and these statutes, to do them: That his heart be not lifted up above his brethren, and that he turn not aside from the commandment, to the right hand, or to the left: to the end that he may prolong his days in his kingdom, he, and his children in the midst of Israel."[32]

Without taking time for contemplation, Michal hefted the heavy scroll upon her shoulder and made her way to the courtyard, where her father reclined beneath an oak tree. She knelt beside him and placed the large volume across his lap.

"Father," she said breathlessly. "Do you remember this scroll, which you penned when first a king?" She did not pause for a response. "Here you copied the word of the Lord and it says, 'And it shall be with him, and he shall read therein all the days of his life: that he may learn to fear the LORD his God, to keep all the words of this law and these statutes, to do them: That his heart be not lifted up above his brethren, and that he turn not aside from the commandment, to the right hand, or to the left: to the end that he may prolong his days in his kingdom, he, and his children, in the midst of Israel.'"[33]

Michal stopped, catching her breath, and watched her father's face. Then she spoke slowly, "Perhaps the blessing of the Lord would return to your life if you would read..."

"No," Saul shouted in a whisper. "Nothing will bring the blessing of the Lord back upon my life."

"But, Father," Michal attempted again.

"Leave me, Michal," Saul said, turning his face away from her. Sadly Michal lifted the scroll and found Zerah at her elbow to take it from her and carry it back up to her rooms.

The days passed into weeks, and when the weeks had passed into months, Jonathan came to the palace and found Michal alone in her rooms, but for the ever present Zerah.

Michal embraced her brother. His face was somber as he led her to a couch and seated himself beside her. "I have news of

---

[32] Deuteronomy 17:14-20

[33] Deuteronomy 17:19,20

David," he told her.

    Michal's eyes watched him and her whole being listened to hear of her beloved. "David fled to Achish, the King of Gath, in Philistia seeking sanctuary. But he did not find safety there and feigned insanity to escape harm.[34] This has come to me." Jonathan showed Michal a scroll, written with close, even script. "David wrote this when he had escaped from the Philistines."

    Michal took the scroll, and holding it toward the light she read aloud.

*Be merciful unto me, O God: for man would swallow
    me up;*
He fighting daily oppresseth me.
Mine enemies would daily swallow me up:
*For they be many that fight against me, O thou most
    High.*
What time I am afraid, I will trust in thee.
*In God I will praise his word, in God I have put my
    trust;*
I will not fear what flesh can do unto me.
Every day they wrest my words:
All their thoughts are against me for evil.
They gather themselves together, they hide themselves,
They mark my steps, when they wait for my soul.
Shall they escape by iniquity?
In thine anger cast down the people, O God.
Thou tellest my wanderings:
Put thou my tears into thy bottle:
Are they not in thy book?
*When I cry unto thee, then shall mine enemies turn
    back:*
This I know; for God is for me.
In God will I praise His word:

---

[34] I Samuel 21:10-15

In the LORD will I praise His word.
In God have I put my trust:
I will not be afraid what man can do unto me.
Thy vows are upon me, O God: I will render praises
unto thee.
For thou hast delivered my soul from death:
Wilt not thou deliver my feet from falling,
That I may walk before God in the light of the
living? [35]

When she had finished reading she clasped it to her breast, bowing her head. Her shoulders trembled with deep emotion. "O, David!" she cried.

"You may keep it," Jonathan said softly. "Read it to feel his presence."

When Michal's grief had subsided, Jonathan told her, "The distressed of Israel, about four hundred men, have rallied to David. Those who are in debt or discontented have followed him and he is their captain. I received news, also, that he has taken his father and mother to Moab for safety,[36] for his grandmother was a Moabitess."[37]

Michal looked into Jonathan's eyes sadly. "Will they ever return to Bethlehem? Will David and I visit them there, again? O, Jonathan why must things be as they are?"

Jonathan folded his sister into his arms as she wept.

Neziah and Merab were both with child, anticipating confinement in the same month. Because Jonathan was often with the troops of Israel, Neziah abode at the palace. Merab, too, came to the palace when her time drew near, for Adriel, also a soldier, was away with the army of Israel.

---

[35] Psalm 56: 1-13

[36] I Samuel 22:3,4

[37] Ruth 4:10,21,22

Michal awaited Merab's arrival anxiously. They had not spoken since the birth of Merab's first child, and then it had been only the necessary conversation in company with others. But now Michal lived at the palace and she and Merab would once again share the rooms where they had been fast friends as children.

Merab's train of servants and guards arrived in the afternoon of a sun drenched day. Michal, too excited to wait in her rooms, descended the stairs and met her in the courtyard. Merab was great with child and the journey had been with much discomfort. The queen and servants descended upon her at once and she was carried to her rooms. They pampered and coddled her, bathing her with cool water and placing her to rest upon soft cushions. Thus, Michal was not able to speak with her alone until all else had receded to leave Merab alone to rest. Michal sat upon a cushion at her side, working a neat row of tiny stitches. Silence reigned as the moments passed.

Michal was the first to speak. "It is good to see you once more, Merab. Your son looks well." She glanced to a sunny spot on the floor where Joel sat and played with carved wooden toys.

Merab smiled toward her son. "Yes," she said tenderly. "He is wonderful, Michal." Then she looked into Michal's eyes with her large blue ones deeply intense. "Do you recall what I told you at your wedding?"

Michal could not endure the penetrating gaze, so looked away. "Yes," she said simply.

"Look at me," Merab implored gently. Michal met her eyes once again. "I was a child, then, Michal. I did not know love. I am now a woman. I now understand love to be giving of oneself. I have learned to love Adriel. There will always be a fondness for David in my heart. But I have let myself learn to be one with my husband, as the Scripture says,[38] and I now know love for Adriel, alone."

"O, Merab," Michal said, dropping her embroidery and taking Merab's hands into hers. "I am happy that you have found love." Her smile faded suddenly and she began to tremble. "I love David dearly, Merab, but our father has driven him away and even now seeks to kill him!"

Merab, with great difficulty because of her expanded frame, put her arms around Michal. She rocked her gently, as a child. "I have heard of Father's malice toward David," Merab said. "It is a wicked spirit, indeed, which defiles our father's soul."

Neziah awoke in travail in the blackness of the night. Ahinoam, Merab, and Michal bathed her brow and spoke soft encouragement to her. The midwives, disheartened, called the physicians, yet, before the dawn broke, Jonathan's daughter was stillborn.

The following night Merab gave birth to a strong, healthy son. She gave him the name of Joshua.

Jonathan returned from the field to comfort his wife. His own grief lay heavy upon him, for he had buried three children, and yet there was not an heir to the throne of Israel. He brought with him another song of David, somehow acquired while in the wilderness. Michal took it to her room to read it alone.

O God, thou art my God; Early will I seek thee:
My soul thirsteth for thee,
My flesh longeth for thee in a dry and thirsty land,
Where no water is; To see thy power and thy glory,
So as I have seen thee in the sanctuary.
Because thy lovingkindness is better than life,
My lips shall praise thee.
Thus will I bless thee while I live:

---

[38] Genesis 2:24

I will lift up my hands in thy name.
My soul shall be satisfied as with marrow and fatness;
And my mouth shall praise thee with joyful lips:
When I remember thee upon my bed,
And meditate on thee in the night watches.
Because thou hast been my help,
Therefore in the shadow of thy wings will I rejoice.
My soul followeth hard after thee:
Thy right hand upholdeth me.
But those that seek my soul, to destroy it,
Shall go into the lower parts of the earth.
They shall fall by the sword:
They shall be a portion for foxes.
But the king shall rejoice in God;
Every one that sweareth by him shall glory: but the
Mouth of them that speak lies shall be stopped.[39]

The beautiful prayer touched Michal's heart. David, a fugitive from the king, still trusted the Lord God without question. He rejoiced in his God. He hoped in his God. Michal bowed her heart before the Lord and prayed. "O God, repay my husband's great faith in You by keeping him safe within Your almighty hands. David praises You, Lord, in his great adversity. Save him from the hand of the king."

Merab rested with her new child, and little Joel napped beside her. Michal slipped from the room and strolled through the cool stone hallways of the palace. As she neared the throne room, she saw that a great throng filled the room and spilled out into the hall. She pressed close and listened to her father's words.

"Hear me now, O Benjamites. Will the son of Jesse give every one of you fields and vineyards, and make you all captains of thousands and captains of hundreds?" The king stood upon

---

[39] Psalm 63

the platform with a spear in hand, gazing over his men, accusation upon his face and in his words. His voice, deep with rebuke, reverberated about the large chamber. "Is this why all of you have conspired against me, and there's no one that shows me that my son has made a league with the son of Jesse? Is this why there's none of you that is sorry for me, or shows me that my son has stirred up my servant against me to lie in wait, as it is this day?"

The men before the king were silent. Indeed Michal felt sorry for the king. Not for the accusation which he had made, but because his wrath against David brought him so low as to make such an accusation. With no answer to give, his men stood speechless before him.

From the rear of the press a voice sounded. "Your Majesty!" A man pushed his way toward the throne and bowed low before the sovereign. As the man stood, Michal recognized him as Doeg, an Edomite whom her father had set over his herdsmen.

"I saw the son of Jesse," Doeg intoned loudly, glancing behind him toward the crowded room. "He went to Nob to speak with Ahimelech the son of Ahitub, the priest. Ahimelech inquired of the Lord for him and gave him food." Doeg paused, glancing once again toward the men behind him. "He also gave him the sword of Goliath the Philistine!" he ended loudly.

Saul stood silent, motionless. His dark, handsome features held no expression which Michal could easily read. When he spoke, his words were smooth as butter, his tone amiable, inviting. "Fetch Ahimelech and all of his father's house, the priests of Nob, here to me. I would receive them here at the palace."[40]

Michal did not know why, but a deep dread rose up in her heart and laid there heavily. She knew that it was unnecessary to

---

[40] I Samuel 22:7-11

summon every priest of Nob for the purpose of discussing David's visit there. A pleasant expression played about her father's face, yet Michal feared an evil design.

CHAPTER 7

THE PRINCESS AND THE EXECUTIONER

"They gather themselves together against the soul of the righteous, and condemn the innocent blood." Psalm 94:21

I am so glad that I was able to come with Mahli to Gibeah," Jehoaddan said lightly. Yet a deep concern etched her voice. "I am so happy to have you. I hope we will have some time to visit. How long can you stay?" Michal asked.

Jehoaddan shook her head. "The messengers from the king didn't say how long the priests would be needed here." The concern now shone from her eyes as well. "They are needed daily for the sacrifices in Nob. My father hopes to return by nightfall."

"Did you see David when he came to Nob?" Michal asked hopefully.

"No..."

A loud shriek cut off Jehoaddan's words. Another scream, and another, followed closely, and then the noise of a great tumult. The two women arose and descended swiftly to the clamor, followed by Zerah. Men and women servants ran screaming through the narrow halls of the palace. Terrified faces and voices swirled about them as they pushed toward the court yard through the current of bodies. Delayed by the press countering them, the two women pushed against the wall, with Zerah before them, protecting them from the terrified throng fleeing from the courtyard.

Forever afterwards Michal was to wish that she and Jehoaddan had not pursued the sounds to the court yard, had not entered there upon such a spectacle as to bring terror to their dreams. Strewn about upon the ground lay the lifeless bodies of the priests of Nob, bathed in their blood which flowed into a river, coursing toward the form of the king of Israel. Saul stood

84

in the midst of the gore, splattered with blood. Beside him stood the herdsman, Doeg, brandishing a sword, crimson with the blood of the men of God who lay at his feet.

Jehoaddan swooned at the sight. Michal caught her friend in her arms and Zerah took her limp form and carried her away. Michal glared at her father. "Why, Father?" she demanded in horror.

"Their hand was with David, and they knew when he fled, and didn't show it to me." Saul's eyes stared past his daughter with a gaze of satisfaction. Michal turned abruptly, her foot slipping in a scarlet puddle. Her father's words stopped her short.

"I have sent a company of armed men to the city of the priests to smite it with the sword." His eyes turned upon her, blazing with passion. "Every man, every woman, every child and infant, all oxen and donkeys and sheep will die!"[41] Saul shouted, triumphant in his victory. Michal turned again and fled the devastation.

Zerah had carried Jehoaddan to Michal's rooms. She lay prone upon the bed, motionless. Yet her eyes were open in horror, staring at nothing. Michal sat upon the bed and stroked her brow, her cheek. The terror of the scene in the court yard had carried Jehoaddan beyond tears. Her grief enshrouded her heart with an impenetrable shield.

"Zerah," Michal addressed the man. "Will Jehoaddan be safe here?"

Zerah pondered the question. "Your father's mind is engaged with his illusion of conquest of his enemy. If she is hidden here, in your rooms, he will not give her mind. I will speak with the servants and they will not reveal her presence."

"Thank you, Zerah. You are such a strength to me." She arose and pulled the big man aside. "Find someone to ride

---

[41] I Samuel 22:6-18

swiftly to Nob. My father has ordered the deaths of all there."

The slave looked soberly into her eyes. "All?" he queried.

"All."

"I will find the best rider and fastest steed at once."

Wagons carried the corpses of the priests, eighty-five in number, to their burial. The servants who were ordered to scrub the blood from the stones of the court yard wept as they worked.

Zerah brought word to Michal that not one servant of Saul had put forth his hand to slay the priests. Doeg, alone, had massacred them. "The king accused Ahimelech of conspiracy against him with David, but the priest pleaded innocence and loyalty to the king. The king answered him that he and all his father's house would die."[42] The strong black man's voice broke, and his shoulders convulsed with emotion.

When the herald returned from Nob, he fell at Michal's feet. His garments were the course sack cloth of mourning, and his head and shoulders were dusted with fine white ashes. So moved with his message was he that only sobs broke forth from his throat. Zerah knelt to comfort the man, and learned from him the awful fate of the city of Nob.

The troops of Saul had reached the city long before the emissary of Michal. As Saul had prophesied, every person, old and young, and every beast in the city had been butchered. The men of Anathoth, a neighboring city, had learned of the massacre at Nob. After the soldiers had departed, they entered the city and began the slow, sorrowful task of burying the families of God's priests.

"I fear for Jehoaddan," Michal told Zerah. Her friend sat in a chair by a window, sun washing over her body, but a shadow shrouding her heart. She had spoken only two words since the slaughter of the priests. "Mahli. Father."

Jehoaddan could not return home, indeed she had no

---

[42] I Samuel 22:11-16

home to which to return. Each day the burden pressed anew upon Michal's heart. Something must be done for her. The palace of Gibeah was an abode of great danger for her. Clutching a missive of David to her breast, Michal walked in the cool twilight of the veranda. The words were engraved upon her heart, so often she had read them. They rose to her lips as a prayer.

> *What time I am afraid, I will trust in thee.*
> *In God I will praise his word, in God I have put my*
>   *trust;*
> *I will not fear what flesh can do unto me.*
> *When I cry unto thee, then shall mine enemies turn*
>   *back:*
> *This I know; for God is for me.*
> *In God will I praise his word:*
> *In the LORD will I praise his word.*
> *In God have I put my trust:*
> *I will not be afraid what man can do unto me.*[43]

Michal found great comfort in the words, not because they were David's words, but because she, too, now trusted God. She didn't know what lay before her, but she knew that she could trust the Lord.

As Michal sat at table with the king and queen, Zerah entered the room and stood behind her couch with arms folded. She glanced at him and he nodded his head slightly.

Michal found meals taken with her parents difficult to ingest. She preferred to take her meals in her rooms, but the king occasionally ordered her to his table. She could not leave until dismissed by King Saul, and he seemed to be in a dark mood, mauling the food upon his plate, reluctant to finish the meal and adjourn the assemblage.

Finally she was released to her rooms. Zerah held his

---

[43] Psalm 56:3-4, 9-11

peace until the heavy door was closed behind them.

Michal stood to face the tall black slave expectantly.

"Princess," he began solemnly. "The son of Ahimelech the priest, Abiathar by name, escaped the slaughter of the priests." He paused, watching hope light in her eyes. "He was aided in escape from the palace and has gone to David."

"David!" Michal exclaimed.

"He has learned of Jehoaddan's presence here, and desires assistance to deliver her from the palace to safety with him. He would take her as his wife, for she is the widow of a priest of the Lord."

Michal glanced toward the room in which Jehoaddan sat, staring out the window. "Does he know...?"

"He knows only that her life is endangered here. The messenger told me that Abiathar himself will wait for her to come to him at a place prescribed. He will go there tomorrow and will wait three days." Zerah watched the face of the princess. "Would the Princess allow her servant to escort the lady hence?"

Michal's eyes burned as an ambition bloomed and grew within her heart. "Yes, Zerah, prepare to leave tomorrow night, with the coming of the darkness." She glanced back toward Jehoaddan. "I will try to explain to her." Then she looked into the eyes of her servant and friend. "And I will go to David."

"Princess, it is far too risky."

"Her life is as precious as mine, indeed more so. I must go to David. I must be with him. I am his wife and we are one. My life is empty and incomplete without him. Zerah, I love David. I shall always love him. I must be with him."

"It would be wiser far to love him from here, and wait until you can safely be together again. I would give my life for you, Princess, but your safety is vital. Please, Princess."

Michal looked away from his intense gaze. "I will go with you."

Soft light of morning stroked Jehoaddan's somber features as Michal sat beside her, caressing her hands. "My dear friend, one of the priests, Abiathar, escaped my father's fury and is safe with David. He has learned of your plight and desires that you go to him and become his wife." Michal watched her friend closely, and saw awareness dawn upon the comely features. Jehoaddan turned her eyes upon Michal for the first time since she had witnessed the murders of her father and husband.

"Abiathar is a good man," she said scarcely above a whisper. "The Lord will give me the grace to accept what I must."

With great relief for the recovery of Jehoaddan and great anticipation of seeing David, Michal bundled clothing and a few necessities into a tight parcel for each. Zerah concealed three mounts and the parcels outside the city walls. The day wore on long for the women who lived for the darkness and escape from the city.

Disguised in hooded robes the two women slipped quietly through a small gate in the palace wall and waited for the slave. The night sounded about them with small rustlings and clickings, causing the two women to gasp, clutching each other closely. A scream almost escaped from Michal's throat as a large shadow loomed before her. Large black fingers pressed gently over her mouth and Zerah's voice said, "It is I, Princess." Zerah led them noiselessly past the slumbering houses to a gate in the city wall. They slipped through and followed a narrow footpath down the side of the mountain in the darkness, Michal clutching Zerah's hand and that of Jehoaddan. The black slave led them away from the path across a field slowly, taking care for brush and stumbling stones. At last they entered the cache where the mounts awaited them. Zerah helped each woman astride a donkey and then mounted and began the ride away from the palace, toward Jehoaddan's waiting bridegroom. Toward David.

The night was perfect for flight, moonless and inky black. Millions of miles up in the ebony sky stars sparkled and watched their escape in passive serenity. They rode in silence, the only sound the rhythmic thud of donkey feet.

Michal's excitement grew. Somewhere ahead Abiathar awaited them and he would lead them to David. This night, before the dawning of another day, she would once again be with David, her love, her husband.

Her life would forever change. David was a fugitive, and she, as his wife, would join in his flight from her father. She would no longer sleep on soft, downy cushions. Her bed would be, perhaps, the ground itself, but it would be David's bed, too. She would learn to cook over an open fire. She would learn to live beneath the sun, her only walls the horizon, her only ceiling the sky. She would learn to live a simple life, frugal and meager. She would learn to care for herself, and indeed, help care for others. The romance of anticipation warmed her in the cool night air. It mattered not what lay ahead, for she would be with David again. Together was enough.

Zerah pulled his donkey to a halt and dismounted. He motioned to the women to stop and wait. He disappeared into a crevice in the rock and a moment later emerged, accompanied by Abiathar, cloaked and leading a mount. Abiathar bowed slightly toward Michal and she nodded. He then approached Jehoaddan, looking up into her concealed face. Soft words were spoken between them. Abiathar mounted his donkey and turned out away from the rocks. Zerah mounted and waited to take up a rearward position.

As Michal gathered up the reins to urge her donkey on, a hand suddenly reached from the darkness and pulled the rein from her, jerking the donkey's head about. Michal was almost unseated, but grasped the neck of the beast to steady herself. The quiet night exploded into a rush of milling soldiers, shouting and crowding closely upon Michal and Zerah.

"Two of them got away!" someone shouted above the din.

"Go after them!" was the bellowed reply.

Helplessly, Michal allowed herself to be led back toward Gibeah, away from David, away from happiness. She could not see her captors in the darkness. She knew that Zerah had fought against restraint, yet to despair. Subdued and bound he walked at her side, head bowed, shoulders sagging.

At the palace, Michal was escorted promptly to her rooms, and the door was secured behind her. Hurtling herself upon her bed, she let go the fountains of her frustration and disappointment. What so little time ago was fervent hope was now dashed into the fragments of desperate sorrow. No tangible thoughts could form in her grief, but images flashed in her mind of a happy and secure Jehoaddan, of a wrathful Saul, of heavy confinement and restriction.

Michal awoke to the light in her room, still clothed in the cloak of her escape, and a rush of remembrance flooded her and weighed against her heavily. David. She should have awakened at his side, in his embrace, this very morning.

She rose and called for Zerah. Two handmaidens, red of eye and sniffing, came at her call.

"Send me Zerah," Michal ordered.

The two young women looked at each other with round eyes and bowed their heads before Michal.

Barely able to form the words, one maid spoke. "Zerah is gone."

"What do you mean?" Michal demanded. "Gone where?"

The girls looked at one another again, and began to weep openly. One girl went to the window and flung open the shutter.

Confused, uneasy, Michal walked to the window and peered toward the gate. She knew when she saw it, but her heart could not receive it. She stubbornly turned and strode to the door, unyielding to the truth before her. Pounding upon the door she ordered. "Open to me!"

A timid response told her, "By order of the king."

"I will deal with the king," Michal demanded. "Open the door."

After a scuffling and whispered argument, the door slowly opened. Michal strode through and descended the stairs.

The maidens and soldiers followed her through the courtyard to the outer gate.

Abruptly Michal stopped. "This is a dream. This is a dream," she told herself. Yet she knew that she indeed stood before the outer gate of the palace courtyard. And there before her, swinging in a passive, slow arc in the slight morning breeze, hung the lifeless form of her guardian, her companion, her friend. The broad shoulders hung, the large gentle hands curled in death, the strong, consoling voice was forever stilled.

"Zerah!" Michal uttered, falling down upon the stones. Great silent sobs shook her. The servants stood about her, dismayed. Michal lifted her tear stained face to a servant. Do not weep before the servants, indeed! And these tears for a slave! Michal quietly asked for sackcloth to be brought to her. Another servant was instructed to fetch ashes from the ovens.

Michal stripped herself of the hooded cloak and the rich garments of royalty, and donned the rough sackcloth. She sat upon the courtyard stones before the hideous pendulum and cast the ashes upon her head and shoulders, and mingled them with her tears upon her face.

Her voice rose in an agonizing wail, lifting to the highest dignity and piercing to the lowest drudge. The city of Gibeah heard the lament and wondered at the palace wall.

"Come, Michal." Gentle hands tried to lift her to her feet, but she pulled away, captive to her anguish. Stronger hands then raised her and carried her away.

Michal numbly submitted to being washed and dressed. She sat in silence, alone, apart, aloof. Surely she now understood madness, indeed partook of it.

Michal refused to eat the food proffered her. She would not sleep, until exhaustion overcame her and prevailed.

When Michal awoke, she remembered all. The flight in darkness, thwarted for her, possibly victorious for Jehoaddan. The murder of Zerah. The empty, hopeless prospect of her life. Then sounded the knock. Could the future be known,

Michal afterward knew she would have cast herself out her window rather than open the door.

Before her stood the king, resplendent in regal attire, attended by a host of servants. He entered her chamber with a flourish. Michal stood mutely. The last time that he had entered here had been one of calamity for Merab. Michal anticipated only malice in her father's presence now.

"Michal, my child," the king cooed. Michal remained silent and still. She had no words for the adversary of her husband and the assassin of her friend.

"It is not good for you to live as a widow here, in the home of your father," Saul was saying.

Michal roused from her lethargy. A wall of defense rose in her heart, fearing imminent attack. She looked into her father's eyes. They smoldered with a fiendish scheme, yet a pleasant smile played upon Saul's handsome features.

"There is a man of Gallim, Laish by name, who has faithfully supplied the armies of Israel with every need, victual and vestment. I would reward his service to the throne." Saul paused. Michal foresaw his words and braced herself. "His son, Phaltiel, has never married. He will come within a week to claim you as his bride."

"I am the wife of David," Michal said firmly.

Saul waved the words away. "He is but a malefactor, fleeing in the wilderness as a dog."

"I am David's wife."

Saul scowled, the pleasant facade giving way to irritation. "David is a dead man. I have no doubt that you will soon be widowed." He again waved at the air. "Regardless, I have voided that bond."

"David and I were joined, not by you, Father, but by the Lord. Neither can you void that bond. I am David's wife."

"You are the daughter of Saul, Sovereign of Israel!" her father pronounced, his volume elevating with each word. "You will do as you are told."

"I am David's wife," Michal declared steadfastly.

Saul squinted at her, rage bringing his breath in angry puffs.

"I have decided," he said fiercely. Turning abruptly, he marched from her chamber.

****

MICHAL, PRINCESS

PART TWO

"Yet the LORD will command his lovingkindness in the daytime, and in the night his song shall be with me, and my prayer unto the God of my life." Psalm 42:8

CHAPTER 8

THE PRINCESS AND THE MERCHANT

"Lover and friend hast thou put far from me, and mine acquaintance into darkness." Psalm 88:18

She refused to alight from the litter. Servants stood about her, perplexed, searching their master's face, awaiting an order. Her father had forced her to enter the litter and leave the palace of Gibeah with this man, Phaltiel. But he could not coerce her to be the man's wife.

"My Lady," the man said, kind pleading in his voice. "The night draws on. Come into the house." He paused and then added very gently, "Please."

"I am the wife of David," Michal said again. It was all that she had said to the man. It was the response she had given to everything he had spoken. She stared straight ahead. As yet she had not even looked at this man.

"You will soon be chilled," Phaltiel said. "Please come into the house."

"Take me back to the palace," Michal ordered.

Phaltiel sighed and glanced about at his servants. Kneeling beside the litter, he reached out a hand to Michal. "Your father would only send you back to me. Please."

At last she looked at him. His hair was very black, and his beard very red. He was small of frame, even frail in appearance. But his green eyes were kind, and he smiled at Michal hopefully.

"I am the wife of David. My father had no right to give me to another." Michal narrowed her eyes and said acidly, "Would you commit adultery with the wife of David?"

Phaltiel sighed again and stood to his feet. "Carry the litter into the house," he commanded the servants. They obeyed straightaway, and Michal was jolted, almost losing her balance.

Before she could breathe a protest, she was carried into the house and the litter was laid upon the floor. She heard the door closed and bolted behind her.

"I am David's wife!" Michal now screamed. "You have no right to bring me here. I demand that you release me!" Receiving no response, Michal peered out from the curtained litter. She saw no one but two sentries posted at the door. Phaltiel was nowhere in sight.

Stepping from the litter, Michal marched to the door. "Open the door," she demanded. The servants stared mutely at the far wall of the room. Grasping the large bolt, Michal attempted to pull it free, but she could not budge it. The two men stood motionless.

Michal turned from the door and looked about the room. There seemed no way of escape. Standing in the midst of the large, ornately furnished room, Michal clenched her fists and shouted to the rafters, "I am the wife of David!" until tears overtook her and she collapsed upon a large cushion.

"My dear," a voice said at her side. She looked up to see an elderly woman, somewhat stooped, holding a small olive oil lamp in one hand, and extending the other toward Michal. "Come with me, now. I will show you your room."

Exhausted in body and mind, Michal obediently followed her up a staircase. The woman stopped at a carved door and reached for the latch. Michal put her hand upon that of the woman. "Phaltiel?" she asked.

"My dear, his room is at the other side of the house. This will be your room."

"Alone?"

"Yes, dear."

Michal entered the room to find there her baggage unpacked and settled in. "I am Hogla, my dear. If you need anything at all, just call me." The woman placed the lamp upon a table, then bowed and backed out of the room. Michal heard the door close and a bolt slide into place.

In a corner near the window, Michal saw the chest in which she kept her mementoes of David. She ran to it and flung herself against it. "David, David," she wept. And there sleep overtook her.

Servants found her prostrate against the chest when they brought to her water for washing in the morning. They stood by silently until she stirred and opened her eyes. Seeing them she rose stiffly, rubbing her neck and shoulders.

"Where are my handmaidens?" she demanded coldly.

The women stood speechless.

"These will be your maids, my lady," Hogla answered her, entering the room with towels and ointments.

"I would have my own maidens," Michal told her stubbornly.

Hogla laid down the burden and looked up at Michal. "The king thought it best for you to have new maids here."

Michal stared bitterly at Hogla. "What is best for me is to be with my husband, David."

"My dear," Hogla said patiently. "You are now the wife of Phaltiel. This is where you belong."

"I am the wife of David," Michal said stubbornly. "Neither my father's word nor that of Phaltiel changes the fact that I am David's wife."

Hogla ceased speaking and turned away. Michal allowed herself to be washed and anointed in silence. When she was dressed and groomed, Hogla returned.

"The master awaits you. You shall break your fast with him."

"I shall not," Michal said, raising her chin. "I will eat here in this room, or I shall eat nothing."

Hogla peered from her heavy lidded, ancient eyes at the princess before her. When she spoke, her words were firm and rang of finality. "Then you shall be hungry, my dear. The master awaits you."

Michal raised her chin anew and followed the woman to

a small, secluded courtyard, lush with verdant foliage and bright flowers. Phaltiel rose to meet her as she came, extending his hands to her. She did not look into his eyes, nor did she acknowledge his greeting. She sat stiffly on the edge of the proffered couch and stared straight ahead.

"You look well, My Lady," Phaltiel said, reseating himself across from her. "I trust that you slept well."

Michal continued to gaze straight before her and did not respond.

Phaltiel lifted a plate of fruits and offered it to Michal. She ignored the gesture.

"Come, now," he said gently. "You must eat, My Lady."

Michal continued her scorn of his attentions.

"This is your home, now, My Lady. I do desire for your comfort and happiness here."

Michal turned her eyes to look into the pleading green eyes of the man beside her. "I am the wife of David," she said without emotion. "I shall be neither comfortable nor happy if I am compelled to remain here."

"My Lady, I do not wish to compel you." Phaltiel said, distress coloring the words. "I hope that you shall learn to be happy here."

"Then I am not your prisoner?"

"Indeed not, My Lady. This is your home."

Ignoring his final remark Michal pursued. "Am I then free to leave?" she asked.

A frown flashed across Phaltiel's lean features. But his eyes did not waver from hers, and his voice was gentle as he asked, "Where would you go?"

Their eyes locked for a moment of silence. Phaltiel spoke. "If you return to your father, he will send you back."

Michal's words were barely audible. "I will go to my husband, David."

Phaltiel smiled wanly. "If the armies of King Saul cannot find David, how would you?"

98

Michal stared across the courtyard to a hummingbird dancing among the bobbing flowers. She lifted her head and swallowed. "I am David's wife," she said.

Phaltiel rose quickly to his feet and strode away from Michal, a slight limp in his gait, stopping beside an ornate flowering bush. He plucked a blossom and pressed it to his nose. When he turned back to her, Michal saw the pain in his features. His voice was strained as he spoke.

"I do not wish for you to be distressed, My Lady. But your father, the king, gave you to me to wife." He approached her and knelt before her, his eyes lowered. "The son of Jesse is no longer confederate with the king. He is an outlaw, a fugitive from the crown of Israel. It is only for your sake, My Lady, that your father has annulled your marriage with such a man."

Michal rose to her feet. "You know nothing of David, what manner of man he is," she told him intensely. "David is a loyal and faithful subject of Israel. He has risked much for the throne and never has he committed ought worthy of anything but praise from the king." Michal looked away from the green eyes and added in a hushed voice, "He loves the Lord God and trusts Him implicitly. Never has he acted against my father, but has ever behaved himself wisely."

Phaltiel stood to his feet and asked quietly, "Are you in love with the son of Jesse?"

"Yes," Michal said with conviction. "I love David dearly. Nothing shall ever alter my love for him." She looked steadily into the eyes of Phaltiel. "And even if David's life were taken, I would never love another."

Silence hung on the fragrant air. The two souls stood together, yet their hearts were remotely separated. The shoulders of Phaltiel sagged in disappointment. Clearly this was not what he had expected when he took the daughter of the king as his wife.

Michal finally spoke, certainty giving her words boldness. "David will come for me, here. I only bide the time until he rescues me and takes me with him."

Phaltiel suddenly bowed low from the waist before her. "My Lady," he said. "I will see to your care and comfort. You have my word that I will not molest you. You will be a guest in my house."

He turned suddenly and strode away, the curious gait slowing his retreat. Michal watched him go and breathed a sigh of relief.

David had transformed Michal's life forever. And here once more, change entered her life. She slowly acquainted herself with the maidens of Phaltiel's house. Hogla's consistent and steady care were comforting. The long, lonely days brought longing for the respite of sleep. Yet, many cries rang through the somber nights as Michal saw in her dreams the pendulous form of Zerah. Hogla silently stroked her brow until the trembling would cease and her breathing quieted.

Michal took her meals in her own room. She sometimes saw the halting form of Phaltiel departing to his business. When he returned it was always with a request for Michal to take the evening meal with him. However, she invariably declined.

She stood before her window, or upon a balcony overlooking the gate to the west of the city. "David," she would whisper into the evening breeze. Then she would lift her voice in prayer. For David. For herself. That the Lord would somehow lead him to her.

To fill the lonesome days, Michal often unsheathed the massive scroll of Saul, poring over the Hebrew characters until her eyes burned. The words became her companion, her consolation.

In Michal's third week at the home of Phaltiel a stranger entered the house, welcomed by the servants. Michal sat upon a balcony with needlework lying idly in her lap.

"Who has come?" Michal asked of Hogla.

"It is your father in law, my dear, the father of Phaltiel. He comes from Michmash where he has been seeing to the supply of the king's troops."

Michal looked intently into Hogla's eyes. "My father in law is Jesse of Bethlehem, the father of David."

"Laish wishes to meet you, my dear."

"There is no need," Michal answered.

"He is the father of Phaltiel."

Upon Phaltiel's return home he himself knocked upon Michal's door. "My Lady," he said, "My father has come. Please attend dinner with me."

"No, I think not," Michal answered.

She heard the man sigh and shift his weight outside the door. "It is only proper that my wife should dine with me."

"I am the wife of David."

"My father only knows that the king of Israel gave to me the hand of his younger daughter in marriage. Please come."

Michal slowly rose and opened the door. She stood once again face to face with the man Phaltiel, the second time only since she had arrived. His green eyes implored for compliance. Michal stepped through the doorway. She did not see the light of hope dawn upon the man's face.

Michal was seated at the table and attended by a host of servants. Laish smiled benevolently at his son and bride.

"Your Majesty," Laish boomed. "It is a great honor to have you in our family." He beamed at Phaltiel.

"I am the wife of David," Michal said.

The smile faded instantly from the face of Laish. He looked at his son uncertainly. Phaltiel's red bearded face flushed crimson in the lamplight. Silence dominated. The meal lay before the three untouched. Servants stood hushed and waiting.

Michal broke the silence, addressing Laish. "I am the wife of David. My father forced me to accompany your son, but I am the wife of David." She gestured toward Phaltiel's bowed head. "Your son has given me his word that I may remain here unmolested." Michal rose from the table and withdrew to her room.

Late into the night Michal could hear the rise and fall of discourse between father and son.

Michal did not see Laish again. He departed, but she did not involve herself. Phaltiel no longer sent to her room to request her presence at dinner.

Wearied by her life of seclusion, Michal left her room to explore the large house in which she lived, careful that Phaltiel had gone. She heard the servants greeting someone at the door, and quickly retreated towards her room.

"My dear, you have a visitor," Hogla called from below. "It is your brother, Jonathan."

Michal gasped, and lifting the hem of her dress, she dashed down. Jonathan stood in the large room where first she had entered the house. Hurling herself into her brother's arms she clung to him desperately. The servants stood by silently, looking away from the lady's tears as she greeted her sibling.

Finally Michal pulled free and led Jonathan to sit upon a large cushion. She ordered refreshment, and servants brought a basin and towel to bathe Jonathan's feet. Michal then dismissed the servants. When they were finally alone she turned anxious eyes upon him.

"Have you heard from David?" were the words she first spoke.

Jonathan's comely face lighted until he fairly glowed a golden blush. "Yes, I spoke with him."

Michal smiled broadly, her first since coming to this house. "What did he say, Jonathan?"

"I found him in the woods of Ziph." Jonathan lowered his eyes. "Our father once again pursued him." He raised his eyes and they smiled again at her. "But the Lord has once more protected David. He and his men rescued the city of Keilah from the Philistines, yet the men of Keilah would have turned him over to the king. The Lord told David to leave and he escaped the king's wrath once again."[44]

"David and I renewed our covenant. The Lord shall make him King of Israel, and I shall be next unto him in the kingdom." Jonathan's voice broke as he spoke these words. He looked at his sister through misted eyes. "I love David better than a brother. My son shall never sit upon the throne of Israel, but I joy in David's prosperity. My happiness is marred only by my father's hatred for the friend of my soul."

"Your son?" Michal asked.

Jonathan smiled broadly again. "Neziah has given me a son at last, Michal. A strong and healthy son from the Lord. God's goodness has no bounds. We have given him the name of Mephibosheth."

"I am happy indeed for you both!" Michal exclaimed, hugging him again. "I will plan to visit Neziah soon."

"Michal," Jonathan said, suddenly sober. "Have you not heard of the queen's illness?"

"What, Jonathan? No one has told me."

"Mother has taken to her bed. The physicians have been called, but they can't find a cure for her malady. You would be as a medicine for her, Michal. Please go to her."

"Yes, I will. I will go tomorrow." Michal grasped Jonathan's hand and squeezed. "Please, Jonathan, promise me something." He nodded. "Find David again. Tell him that I am still his faithful wife. This man Phaltiel has not touched me. I still wait for David to come and take me away from here with him. Will you tell him, Jonathan?" Sister and brother locked eyes in understanding.

"I promise to tell him when next the Lord grants me privilege to see him."

Phaltiel escorted Michal to the palace of Gibeah attended by servants. Outwardly they were husband and wife. Only the

---

[44] I Samuel 23:13

servants of Phaltiel knew differently.

The visit was one of pain. Entering through the gate where last she had seen her beloved servant Zerah was sorrowful for Michal. Seeing the rooms where she and David had been together filled her with melancholy.

And her mother, the queen, was ill. She lay in her bed, propped by many cushions, and attended by anxious servants. She smiled wanly as Michal sat at her side. In her feeble state she still held her head high, and the regal air pervaded the room about her. Michal spent the majority of time at her mother's side.

When Phaltiel returned to the palace to fetch Michal back to his home, she considered refusal, insistence upon remaining at the palace. But her mother was very ill and her father angry and preoccupied. She entered the litter of her own accord.

"Sir," she said.

Phaltiel turned, his green eyes eagerly seeking hers. "My Lady?"

"I would go visit my brother's wife, Neziah, who has just been delivered of a son." She watched the frown flicker across Phaltiel's features. "I would also visit my sister in Gilgal."

"You would return home?"

"Where could I go?"

"My lady, I go to the feast in a fortnight. I desire that you accompany me." Phaltiel watched her closely, waiting breathlessly. "I will return in time to go to the Tabernacle."

Once released at Jonathan's home, Michal felt as the girl she had once been. She and Neziah chatted comfortably about babies and cooed and adored the infant prince. Jonathan found time to take leisure at home and talk with his sister. With him her every conversation turned to David.

"And what of Phaltiel?" Jonathan asked one sun drenched afternoon as they lay lazily in the shade, fanned by servants.

"What of him?" she asked.

"He has taken you to wife. If David cannot rescue you..."

"David will come!" Michal sat bolt upright. "He loves

me, Jonathan. He will find a way to get into the city of Gallim and take me away from Phaltiel's home." She stared away from her brother's gaze. "He must."

"David's life is not one of ease, little sister," Jonathan told her. "It is a big job to feed and protect a band of four hundred men and their families. And he must ever be watchful for his life."

"His men have their families with them. I care not if the way be difficult, Jonathan. I belong with David."

"It would be extremely dangerous for him to go to Gallim."

Michal stood to her feet. She lifted her chin and glared down at her brother. "David will find a way!" she declared, and marched away into the house.

Reluctant to leave her brother's home, yet eager to see her sister, Michal endured the rough trip to Gilgal. Her train trailed far along the road, consisting of guards and servants, victuals, baggage, and gifts for Merab.

The city of Gilgal was much smaller than Gallim. Michal's heart stung with memories of the small city of Bethlehem, to which she and David had travelled. But when she saw her sister, with two small boys clutching at her skirts, her heart reached out to Merab. Merab, great with child, greeted her lovingly.

"I am always ready to deliver a child when you see me!" Merab exclaimed. She introduced Michal to her small nephews and they shyly greeted her, then scampered away to play.

"Michal it is so wonderful to see you!" Merab exulted. Her brows knit in a cautious frown. "I heard of your marriage to the son of Laish."

"It is no marriage. I am David's wife. I wait faithfully for David to take me away with him."

Merab considered Michal for a moment. "Sometimes it is a woman's place to accept..."

"I am David's wife!" Michal said fiercely.

Merab took her sister's hand into her fading lap and patted it. "It is good of Phaltiel to be so patient with you, Michal."

Michal looked at her sister in astonishment. "He has no choice. I am the wife of David!"

"Didn't our father give you to Phaltiel to wife?"

"Yes, but..."

"Then he does have a choice little sister." The two sat quietly, looking into one another's eyes.

Michal changed the subject of conversation. "How is it with you, Merab?"

Merab smiled and laid her arm across her swollen belly. "Adriel is good to me." A cloud passed over her sun. "He is gone so very much of the time, though, that the boys must reacquaint themselves with him each time he returns. They are so small, you see."

Michal laid her hand upon her sister's belly and said playfully, "He comes often enough I would say."

The time passed all too quickly for Michal, but she had promised to return for the feast. Tears parted the sisters as Michal rode away from Gilgal.

Saul had moved the Tabernacle from the ravaged city of Nob to the high place at Gibeon, a high, rounded mountain which afforded a panorama in every direction. The citizens of Gibeon were a Canaanite people, servants to the priests of Israel, hewing and carrying wood and drawing water for the services of the altar of God. Long ago in Israel's history the Gibeonites had deceived the man of God, Joshua, and the nation of Israel had made league with them.[45] But Saul, in his great zeal to eliminate the traitorous priests, had also massacred the Gibeonites living in Nob. So, in attempt to appease the enraged leaders of Gibeon, he placed the Tabernacle there.

---

[45] Joshua 9:3-15,23

Phaltiel, with Michal at his side, presented his offering before the Tabernacle. Priests which Saul had ordained to the office offered the sacrifice of blood upon the altar. Yet, the ceremony seemed empty and lifeless. Michal recalled the offering of David, the strong hands so gently caressing the lamb before the blade was applied, the tears of grief over his iniquities before his God.

Michal endured the feasting which followed Phaltiel's sacrifice. They sat atop the hill at long tables spread with sumptuous fare. Michal's eyes scanned the horizon, hopeful that David would somehow know that she was there. Anticipation churned her stomach, as she imagined his charge up the hillside, his gallant rescue as he took her upon his steed and galloped away. But the sun set upon the feast without David, and Michal went to her tent greatly disappointed and sorrowful.

When the train of Phaltiel reached his house in Gallim upon returning from the feast, Michal hurried to her room and drew from the chest her treasures of David. For a night and a day she sat holding them against her heavy heart. Again and again she read the prayers to God, written by his own hand. She refused food and drink and dismissed all servants from her room. "David, David," she cried over and over.

Michal awoke and rose stiffly. Her well was dry of tears. She gently placed David's small harp and sling into the chest beside the well worn scrolls and closed the lid. She allowed the servants to bathe and feed her. Her mind was turned inward with great self pity when suddenly Jonathan stood at her door.

Taking her hands in his he stood in silence. Fear shadowed Michal's heart. "David?" she asked.

Jonathan shook his head slowly. He frowned and she knew that he was troubled to frame the words. "Our father has taken a woman to his comfort," he said simply.

"And our mother?" she asked in alarm.

"She lives, Michal. She is ill, but she lives."

All of Michal's self pity transformed instantly into rage.

"I shall go at once to the palace," she said. Jonathan still held her hands and did not release them.

"You could gain nothing by incurring the king's wrath," he told her.

She raised her chin in defiance of the threat. "Neither is there anything to lose."

CHAPTER 9

THE PRINCESS AND THE DEFENDER

"When my father and my mother forsake me, then the Lord will take me up." Psalm 27:10

The servants nervously watched their mistress leave with Jonathan, for their master was away, and knew not of his wife's departure.

Michal marched into the presence of the King of Israel. He reclined on a sunny porch, alone. He rose to greet his daughter, but she ignored his salute. "What have you done to my mother?" she demanded.

"My child," Saul answered her graciously. "Your mother is ill. I have done nothing at all to her."

"You have taken a harlot to yourself, and in my mother's home."

Saul smiled benignly at his daughter and shook his head. "No, my child, a concubine. I am a sovereign, am I not? It is the custom for a sovereign to satisfy himself with concubines."

"The custom of the heathen, Father," Michal said coldly. "The Lord God has commanded that a king shall not multiply wives unto himself."[46]

Saul scowled and pushed away her words with his hand. "The Lord God cares not with whom I make my bed," Saul said sullenly. "The Lord God cares neither for my life nor my soul."

Michal stared at her father. She knew that he had once trusted the Lord. But now he spoke as an infidel. Was his sin so great that he could deny his God?

Michal started as a fair young woman entered the porch. She was young, indeed no older than Michal. She stood quietly,

---

[46] Deuteronomy 17:17

108

sheathed in veils, yet Michal perceived a slim body and lovely countenance.

"Come, Rizpah," Saul invited, extending his hand to the young woman.

She stepped toward him, but Michal barred the way. "Go, you whore!" Michal shouted at her. She raised her hand to strike Rizpah, but Saul's strong grasp prevented her.

"My daughter, Michal," he said calmly. "She was just leaving."

Michal gave her father a last icy stare and turned to leave. His parting words to her cut to her heart. "My child, do not judge your father, when you yourself have gone to another man's bed."

Michal ran, blinded by her tears, through the palace halls. The servants, who knew her well, could only step aside and let her pass; but their hearts ached for their princess. She sought Jonathan, but found at the palace gate the solemn form of Phaltiel

Seeing her tears, Phaltiel reached for her, exclaiming in alarm, "My Lady!"

She stopped just short of his grasp.

"Is it your mother?" he asked in concern.

"It is my father!" she shouted at the man. "My father accuses me of infidelity to my husband, to cover his sin."

Phaltiel did not move. His green eyes watched her with great sorrow. "I know that you are a true wife to David," he said sadly.

Michal stood before the man Phaltiel and remembered the words of her sister. Yes, he was a good man, indeed, to so kindly allow her to be faithful to David.

"Thank you," she whispered to him. "Please take me home."

Michal did not accompany Phaltiel to the Tabernacle when next he must go. All the men of Israel were required by the law of the Lord to appear before the Tabernacle three times a year.[47]

Phaltiel allowed Michal to travel to Gilgal for the confinement of Merab. She was delivered of another son, healthy and strong. He was circumcised on the eighth day and given the name of Jashub. Michal stayed with Merab the forty days until she went to the Tabernacle to offer there her sacrifice, as commanded in the law of God.[48] Adriel had returned and escorted his wife to do her duty before the Lord.

Before returning to the home of Phaltiel, Michal travelled to Gibeah to visit Jonathan once more. She joyed in Jonathan's healthy child, Mephibosheth. Jonathan drew her apart privately and confided the latest news of David.

"Our father once again seeks David at Maon. Here," Jonathan handed to her a small scroll, crimped and soiled. "this is another missive of David."

Michal looked anxiously at Jonathan. "You told David, didn't you, that I still await him, that I am a true wife to him?"

"We met for only a moment. We could speak of nothing, but to cheer each other's heart in the Lord." The man looked at his sister with compassion. "Don't lose hope, little sister. Take this. Read it and know that David is in the hands of the Lord."

Michal went into the open courtyard and seated herself beneath a fruited tree. Carefully she unrolled the tightly coiled document. Tears streamed as she read the short prayer.

Save me, O God, by thy name, and judge me by thy
strength.
Hear my prayer, O God; give ear to the words of my
mouth.
For strangers are risen up against me, and oppressors
seek after my soul:
They have not set God before them. Selah.

---

[47] Exodus 23:17

[48] Leviticus 12:4,6

Behold, God is mine helper: the Lord is with them that
    uphold my soul.
He shall reward evil unto mine enemies: cut them off
    in thy truth.
I will freely sacrifice unto thee: I will praise thy name,
O LORD; for it is good.
For he hath delivered me out of all trouble: and mine
    eye hath seen his desire upon mine enemies.[49]

"David!" she cried in anguish. "David! When will you
come? When will you take me away with you?" She fell upon
the couch and wept bitterly.

The seed of a plan was conceived that day, and continued
to grow in Michal's heart. It was true, as Jonathan had said, that
David would face great danger to come to Gallim to rescue her.
She had endangered and wasted Zerah's life in trying to go to
David. "I will go alone," she mused silently throughout the long,
lonely days.

Michal descended the stairs and presented herself to
Phaltiel as he sat at his table for the evening meal. Delight lit his
eyes as he rose and seated her at his side. Michal gave no
explanation for her sudden appearance. She said little, but
listened attentively as the man talked to her. He was genuinely
enraptured to have her present. She nodded and smiled slightly
in response to his dialogue, yet her ears were carefully tuned to
detect any hint to aid her in her escape. Yes, he spoke to her of
his business, his plans. Yes, he told her that he must be away for
several days, soon, to aid his father in the business in Michmash.
He smiled at her and promised an effort to return as soon as
possible.

Michal attended the evening meal with Phaltiel each day
until his departure. The man left with hope in his heart, she
knew, and a small pang shot through hers. But very small, for

---

[49] Psalm 54

she would find her way to David, and this nightmare of separation would end.

Michal made careful note of the whereabouts of each household servant, and knew that each was occupied. Hogla oversaw the women at the large iron kettles, stirring the pungent soap over the low flames. None was aware as Michal donned the hooded cape of the infamous night of prior escape and slipped out the gate. She hurried along the street to the gate of the city, and with the hood masking her face, she slipped through and onto the road going south.

Fellow travellers passed her without a word, some upon beasts and many on foot. They all, it seemed, could walk along the rough, hilly road far faster than she. By the time she had gone what she determined to be an hour, she was winded and perspiring beneath the heavy cape. Her feet, shod in delicate slippers, ached, and she felt blisters budding. She left the road and seated herself beneath a fig tree, which spread its branches invitingly to the traveler. The shade eased her as she drew a drink from a flask drawn from the folds of the cape. Squinting into the horizon Michal divided the ribbon of road before her into segments such as she had already come. Hours. It would take hours to reach the hill before her in the distance. Yet, she knew that she must continue, day and night, until she found David.

Michal made herself begin again, and as she walked along, she found that her feet grew numb and ceased their aching, and that she could cover a great distance unaware of the throb in her legs if she directed her thoughts to David. Her weary body trudged on as her mind whirred. David! It had been so long since she had seen the love in his blue eyes, felt the strength of his arms around her, heard the music of his voice.

She found herself reciting the poetic prayers of David, and drew comfort from the words.

"Save me, O God, by thy name, and judge me by thy strength. Hear my prayer, O God; give ear to the words of my mouth...Behold, God is mine helper: the Lord is with them that

uphold my soul...For he hath delivered me out of all trouble: and
mine eye hath seen his desire upon mine enemies."[50]

    She hummed a tune of David to herself and the words
formed in her heart and escaped from her lips. "The Lord is my
shepherd, I shall not want..."[51]

    The western sky was streaked with red and gold when
Michal finally let herself stop and rest again. She pulled a parcel
from her cloak and had a repast of bread and cheese, pilfered
from the kitchen of Phaltiel's house. Every muscle ached, even
ones she never before knew she possessed. She lay her head
back against a rock and closed her eyes. She did not intend to
sleep, but the fatigue overwhelmed her and the soothing arms of
slumber beckoned and welcomed her.

    A fierce grasp rudely awakened her. Blinded by the
darkness and confused by the sudden assault, Michal flailed with
her arms and kicked her attacker violently. Freed by her
intensity, she lifted the weighty skirt of her robe and ran into the
blackness. But her pursuer was swifter than she, and a heavy
blow knocked her to her knees before him. Michal was aware
that several bodies circled her in the ominous blackness. Rough
hands pulled her to her feet, and pushed into the robe, seeking
gold, or jewels, or what?

    A sudden clamour encompassed them. Torches blazed
and drew flashes across the darkness as horsemen charged into
the fray. Shouts and shrieks echoed into the night. Michal was
released, and she crouched into a ball on the ground, unable to
move.

    The bandits, wounded and bleeding, retreated hastily
among the trees. Seeing them flee, Michal stood. Grasping her
skirts she began to race furiously along the road.

    A horseman approached her, his steed prancing at her

---

[50] Psalm 54:1,2,4,6

[51] Psalm 23:1

side. She dashed away from the road, up a slight incline. The strength drained from her as she ascended the rough ground, and she stumbled, falling upon her face on the ground. Desperately, she rose to her hands and knees and crawled, her legs tangling in the long skirts.

She heard the horseman, now on foot, climbing the hill behind her.

"My Lady!" a familiar voice called tremulously. "My Lady, it is I, Phaltiel!"

Michal slumped into a heap on the ground, sobs of exhaustion and relief racking her body. Phaltiel gently lifted her, and she clung to him. He held her against him thus until the sobs subsided and the trembling eased. Then he lifted her and carried her down the slope to his waiting steed. Mounted servants held torches, eerily lighting the scene. Phaltiel lifted Michal to his horse and mounted behind her. They rode in silence back along the miles which Michal had traversed that long and weary day. Finally Phaltiel spoke.

"I will take you to David."

Michal started and tried to turn and see his face in the darkness. "Why would you take me to David?" she asked gently.

"You are determined to go to him. You might have been killed." His voice trembled.

David! Phaltiel would take her to David!

"How would you find him?" she asked.

"What was your plan to find him?" the man asked.

Silence reigned in the dark night, but for the prancing of the horses' feet.

"But you will try?" Michal asked.

"I pledge myself to deliver you to your husband," Phaltiel answered, a depth of sorrow in the words.

Dawn approached as the band neared the city of Gallim. The watchmen at the gate opened at the voice of Phaltiel. In the courtyard of Phaltiel's home servants rushed forward to aid. As Michal was lifted down she felt a cool dampness against her back. She brushed her hand across the dampness and when she looked, it was crimson. Blood! Phaltiel had dismounted and now slumped against a servant.

"The master is wounded!" someone shouted. They carried Phaltiel into the house and laid him upon a couch. Hogla hurried in and tore aside his garments, revealing an ugly gash across his chest. Swiftly, yet gently and with great care, Hogla washed the wound. A servant brought a steaming bowl, and Hogla applied the contents. Phaltiel, who lay with eyes closed and the pallor of death upon his face, groaned. Soft dressings were applied and his torso was wrapped securely.

Only then did Hogla look at Michal, who hung in the shadows at Phaltiel's side. Hogla's eyes squinted in the lamplight, and she pursed her mouth. When her words came, they were gravel against Michal's ears. "The master risked his life to save you. And he may lose it, yet."

Chastened by the old woman's eyes and words, Michal spoke softly. "I'm grateful for his deliverance from the thieves. I do not wish him harm." She glanced away from the stony gaze toward the wounded man. "Why did he come? How did he know?"

"When we knew that you had gone," Hogla said, the icy words stinging in Michal's ears, "a servant rode fast to Michmash to tell the Master. He left immediately and followed the road south from Gallim." Hogla reached a clawlike hand to grasp Michal's arm, pulling her gaze to her own. "The Master knew that you would be in great danger upon the road alone." Hogla released her grip and looked at Phaltiel, pale beneath the blazing lamps. The ice melted from her voice and she spoke tenderly.

"The master has never been strong. His dear mother, my beloved mistress, perished from a plague which gripped both her and her child. He was so small and frail, yet he lived. His limbs are thin and feeble, but his heart has great courage and strength." Hogla looked again at the princess. Her aged eyes sagged from sorrow. "I love him as a son. It grieves me much to see him harmed, in body," the old woman paused, "or in spirit."

Michal stayed at the side of Phaltiel, bathing his brow, speaking soft encouragement through the frightful hours which followed. She did not eat nor sleep, until Hogla compelled her to leave the man's side and find rest. But sleep was not restful for Michal, for she dreamed the nightmare of her attack by the thieves and her rescue, to find Phaltiel torn open, bleeding, yet with gentle eyes beseeching her. She awoke in terror, drenched with sweat, and returned to his bedside vigil.

Physicians were sought, who administered salves to the gaping wound. Yet, it was the gentle care of Hogla which seemed to ease him most.

Michal awoke with a start from dozing at Phaltiel's bedside. She peered anxiously at the man, for he seemed too quiet. She leaned close to detect breath, and was assured by the soft rush of air. She sat quietly, watching his peaceful sleep.

Phaltiel's eyes watched Michal for several moments before she realized that he had awakened. She was suddenly shy before his gaze, and looked quickly away.

"My Lady," Phaltiel said in a half whisper.

Michal looked back at the man. He raised himself up in the bed on one elbow. His green eyes smiled. "Are you well, My Lady?"

"I?" she asked, perplexed.

"The thieves did not harm you?"

Michal smiled in comprehension. "They did not harm me. How do you feel?"

Phaltiel frowned slightly. "I feel somewhat dizzy," he answered, attempting to rise. With a groan he fell back onto the bed.

"Oh, please do not try to rise. You were injured. The thieves...don't you remember?"

Phaltiel closed his eyes. "Yes, I remember." He opened his green eyes and they searched hers. "How long?"

"You have been ill for five days."

Neither spoke for several moments. Michal wondered if she should call Hogla and report Phaltiel's waking. But she sat quietly at his side.

"When I have mended I will take you to David," Phaltiel said suddenly, rising upon his elbow again.

Michal's heart leapt. David! But as she watched the man before her, she knew that it could not be done.

"What would be the response of the king, my father, if you were to take me to David?"

"I would risk anything for your happiness, My Lady."

"You have already risked your life once for my sake. I can't let it happen again." Michal looked away from the intense emerald gaze.

"Then I shall send emissaries to find David, with a message from me. I shall tell him that you are a true wife to him, and that you await reunion with him." Phaltiel's voice was cheerless.

"Why would you do such a thing for me?" Michal asked.

Phaltiel remained silent for a moment, resting upon his elbow. His eyes pools of deep sadness, he replied. "I am but one of your servants, My Lady. But you are all to me. I wish only for your contentment."

Her circumstances were unique, yet Michal knew that such devotion for another man's wife was improper. Still, she felt that this man's heart was pure in motive and esteem.

"I shall call Hogla," she told him. "She will be happy to see you awake."

Three men were sent with the missive for David. Saul's men had indeed had difficulty locating David in the wilderness where he concealed himself and his four hundred men and their families. Yet, Michal's heart was full of hope for the three emissaries.

The days of waiting made Michal edgy. Phaltiel was mending well and able to get up and around the house, so she asked leave to visit the queen.

The faint light in the bed chamber of Ahinoam veiled the paleness of her visage, but as Michal held her thin, blue veined hand, she felt the shadow of death lurking in the corners of the room. The queen tried to smile and speak of pleasant things.

"Your sister will be delivered of another child, shortly," the queen told her.

"So soon?" Michal said, dismayed. "I should go and visit her, again." Even as she spoke the words, Michal knew that she may never again see her sister, or her mother. She would very shortly be with her husband, and he was a fugitive from her father's domain.

Michal lingered at her mother's side as much as possible. On the afternoon of the third day she stepped onto the veranda for a respite in sunshine and peace. A memory accosted her with a wave of longing, of a shepherd musician's voice raised in devotion to the Lord, of his eyes searching those of a suddenly shy princess, here in this very spot. Her eyes misted at the recollection and her heart yearned for David.

"Michal, my child!"

Michal whirled to find her father, reclining behind her, concealed by a column.

"I am glad to see you! I heard that you were in the palace and had so hoped to have you take your meals at the royal table."

"I have come to see my mother," Michal answered, her gaze into her father's eyes unwavering.

"That is good," Saul cooed. "Ah, my sweet Rizpah!" Saul turned to greet his concubine, and Michal instantly retreated. As she passed the slight figure of the king's diversion, she noticed the belly, swollen with child. King Saul did not try to call her back.

Because she would soon receive the message from David telling her his plans to rescue her, or to meet her, or to send deliverance to her, Michal tried to be especially kind to the man who had shown her such benevolence. She visited him as he rested on his veranda. She took her meals with him. She knew he suffered a great grief because she would go to David. He smiled at her and spoke casually of trivial matters, but she knew his heart was breaking.

Michal spent much of her time on a small balcony overlooking the courtyard where the emissaries would return with a message from David. David! The very thought of him thrilled her. At long last she would be at his side once more. Life would once again be good to her.

The days passed slowly, and a fear began to gnaw the edges of Michal's hope. "David is hidden well," she told herself. "They will find him. I will be with him, again."

A messenger arrived, heralding the birth of Merab's son. He had been given the name of his father, Adriel. Michal wept in her room at the news of the child and the sister she would never again see. She dared not leave the home of Phaltiel again, for the emissaries were sure to arrive soon.

"But I cannot leave here," Michal told Phaltiel one morning as they sat breaking their fast. "They will surely return while I am absent."

Phaltiel raised a goblet to his lips, keeping his eyes fixed on hers. "The king will expect you to be present. We have been summoned to travel with the king's train to Ramah to lament the man of God, Samuel. You will be sorely missed if you don't attend. And you will see your sister once more," the man ended gently.

Michal looked away from him. It was true that she must attend the burial of Samuel. She rose and paced the pavement. She must not miss the message from David. Surely they would soon find David and bring to her the news of hope which she anticipated so eagerly.

The ride to Ramah was pleasant enough. Michal was carried in a curtained litter, and refreshment was at her side throughout the journey. But she pulled back the curtain and her eyes strained into the horizon toward Gallim. When Gallim had passed from sight, she lay back against the cushions and wept.

120

Michal suddenly sat upright. Her troubled heart implored the God of heaven. "Oh, Lord, please hear my prayer. Do not let me miss the message from David. I must be with David, again. Lord God, You are the only One who can put us together once more."

All Israel came to Ramah to lament the death of the great prophet of God. Michal wondered at the great sorrow which King Saul bore before the tomb of Samuel. His children came to his aid as he prostrated himself there upon the earth. Tears streaked his face as he looked at his sons and daughters.

"Samuel was my only link with God," Saul whispered hoarsely. "Now that he is gone, all hope is gone."

Jonathan's grip upon his father's arm tightened. "O my God, I trust in thee: let me not be ashamed, let not mine enemies triumph over me," Jonathan quoted. "Yea, let none that wait on thee be ashamed: let them be ashamed which transgress without cause. Shew me thy ways, O Lord; teach me thy paths. Lead me in thy truth, and teach me: for thou art the God of my salvation; on thee do I wait all the day." [52]

Michal watched her brother, eyes wide, heart thumping. Those were words such as David composed. Jonathan glanced at her and nodded.

The words did not assure the heart of Israel's king. He clutched at his children and cried, "But the Lord no longer hears my prayers! The Lord has estranged Himself from me!"

Some stared, yet many delicately turned their gaze aside, as the King of Israel, once tall and powerful, strong and handsome, was led from the graveside of Samuel, a shattered man.

Jonathan had slipped the latest song of David into Michal's hand before her departure from Ramah. She pored over the words as the litter carried her back to the home of Phaltiel.

---

[52] Psalm 25:2-5

Shutting her eyes hard against the light, Michal prayed some of David's words.

"Turn thee unto me, and have mercy upon me; for I am desolate and afflicted. The troubles of my heart are enlarged: O bring thou me out of my distresses. Look upon mine affliction and my pain; and forgive all my sins... O keep my soul, and deliver me: let me not be ashamed; for I put my trust in thee."[53]

Michal waited. She had seen her family, one and all, for the final time. She was ready to go to David. She packed a small collection of clothing and such things which she deemed suitable to a life in the wilderness. She read and reread the songs and prayers of David until each one was firmly embedded in her heart. She paced the floors of the house, wringing her hands.

Hearing a visitor speaking with a servant at the door, Michal hurried in excitement, but was disappointed to find a messenger from the palace of King Saul. The man placed a roll into her hand, and bowing before her, took his leave. Michal opened the roll and read a message by the hand of her father.

"I wanted you to know, my dear child, of the birth of my son, Armoni." That was all. Michal handed the roll to the servant and told him to burn it.

Michal was pacing her room when Hogla called her to Phaltiel. She found him standing in the small garden with three men. Her heart skipped a beat as she recognized them and she hurried to Phaltiel's side. She could not understand the kindness in Phaltiel's smile nor the gentle way in which he seated her, sitting beside her.

Michal looked at the men and then at the man Phaltiel. She spoke one word, "David?"

Phaltiel glanced at the messengers and sighed. His mild green eyes looked at hers sadly, yet she knew it was not sadness for himself.

---

[53] Psalm 25:16-18,20

122

"These men sought David long and hard," he said. Michal nodded, waiting. "They did not speak with him in person, but they met some of his men in the wood."

"The message, they sent the message to David?"

Phaltiel hesitated. "The men said that David had heard that your father had given your hand in marriage...to me." Michal's heart was pounding wildly. "David has remarried. He has taken two more wives."[54]

Michal's heart continued to beat hard against her ribs. She knew what Phaltiel had told her, but comprehension was slow in coming, and denial came with it.

"No!" she said firmly. "I am David's wife. I have waited faithfully." She looked beseechingly into the eyes of the man who knew all too well that she spoke truthfully. His face softened further, but he did not respond.

"No!" Michal shouted, rising to her feet. "No! I am David's wife!" Lifting her skirts she fled the room.

---

[54] II Samuel 25:42-44

CHAPTER 10

THE PRINCESS, THE WIDOW

"The LORD preserveth the strangers; he relieveth the
fatherless and widow: but the way of the wicked he turneth
upside down." Psalm 146:9

Darkness descended and settled about Michal as a shroud.
She ordered a dress of black and secluded herself. Food
was carried to her room as before, and the dishes were
returned to the kitchen untouched. Michal would not allow the
sunlight into her room, but the windows were tightly shuttered.

David. A single thread of thought wound its way through
Michal's wounded mind and heart. David. She lay prone for
hours holding that one thought. She sat cross legged before the
chest of David, running her fingers against the smooth woodgrain
and the rough leather latch until her fingers oozed and her blood
smeared with her strokes. She did not open the chest. She could
not look upon the shepherd's garb and sling or the well worn
harp. Her heart could not bear the words penned with such care
upon the parchments. David.

The man Phaltiel came regularly to her room to ask after
her welfare, but she did not speak with him. Hogla would step
outside and converse with him in muted tones, and he would
finally leave.

The days passed dully, each as the one before. Michal
grew thin and gaunt. Hogla coaxed beverage and broth between
her reluctant lips, but after only a few spoonsful Michal would
turn her face away.

The lonely vigil of Michal may well have persisted until
she faded from life. But her seclusion was suddenly invaded by
a visit from Jonathan. She allowed herself to be washed and
groomed, and exited her room for the first time since her
bereavement.

"Michal!" Jonathan exclaimed in shock at her pale waxlike features veiled in black. He took her into his arms and held her close. "Does he treat you ill?" he asked.

Michal clung silently to Jonathan for a moment. Pulling back to see his face she shook her head. "I am well treated and cared for here."

Jonathan searched her eyes. "Are you ill?"

Michal averted her eyes and said in a tone low and sad, "My pain is not outward, but in the heart."

"The black. Are you in mourning?"

She looked back into his eyes. "Have you seen David?"

"No, little sister. I have been with the troops of Israel, but not those seeking David."

"Have you heard, Jonathan?"

"Heard about David?"

"He knows that Father gave me to this man Phaltiel. David has taken two wives." Michal's voice broke and she fell against her brother, weeping. Through her tears she sobbed, "I have been a faithful wife to David! I have waited for him to rescue me and take me with him."

"And Phaltiel?"

"Phaltiel has shown nothing but kindness and respect for another man's wife."

Jonathan rocked her gently back and forth and let her weep. When he spoke his voice was gentle and undaunted. "David would not wrong you." He held her away from him and made her look into his face. "You must believe, Michal, that David would have come for you long since if it were possible. He is a hunted man. Our father seeks his life passionately. When he heard that you were given to another man he could not know that Phaltiel would allow you to remain faithful to him. You must understand, little sister, that he took another wife only because he believed you were lost to him."

"Two other wives," Michal said bitterly.

"I came to bring you news of him," Jonathan said

hesitantly. "I did not know... The Ziphites told the king that David and his men were in the hill of Hachilah. Our Father sought him there. As the king and his troops slept, David crept to his side and took his spear and a cruse of water that lay near him. David called to the king and begged to know for what evil he was pursued." Jonathan's voice trembled. "Our Father confessed his sin to David and swore to do him no more harm."[55]

Tears were in his words as he continued. "Michal, the heart of our Father has hardened as iron before the Lord. He might well have meant his confession to David. But I would not trust him to remember that repentance. Our Father's soul is in the grasp of evil..." He broke, and together they wept, one for the king, one for the fugitive.

When their tears had passed, Michal led Jonathan to the small garden and there they sat. Servants came without sound and washed the feet of Jonathan. Trays of fruits and cool drinks were carried to them. No words passed between them until all activity ceased and the servants melted away into the shadows.

Jonathan stroked Michal's frail hand with his thumb. "Little sister," he said gently. "do you persist still in tarrying for David?"

Her eyes animated suddenly as passionate words passed from her lips. "David is dead to me. I am no longer a wife, but a widow."

She watched Jonathan's fair face but could read nothing in his azure eyes. His yellow beard began to bob lightly. "David is dead to you."

"Yes."

"Then you are free to remarry."

Michal frowned, hardly seeing the point of the subject.

"You have told me that Phaltiel has been only kind and gracious to you. I know hardly a man who would take a wife,

[55] I Samuel 26:21

whatever her circumstances, and not take her unto himself. I
have only the acquaintance of the man, but, little sister, I believe
him to have a good heart. I deem that he must hold you in high
regard."

Michal did not respond. Her gaze did not leave his
handsome face.

"Consider, if you will, the man Phaltiel as a husband,
indeed. I believe he would attempt all within his power to make
you happy."

Love knit the sibling hearts as they sat thus in silence. A
tiny breeze played a wisp of hair across Michal's face. She
pushed it away and lifted her chin high. "I will consider it."

Delight lit the face of Phaltiel as Michal entered the room
in which he sat to take his repast. He stood suddenly and seated
her beside him. She saw in his eyes a great concern for her
fragile frame of body and mind. She knew that he noticed the
change of apparel; no longer did she wear the habit of mourning.

"My Lady, you pleasure me much to join me for supper."
He smiled and passed to her a platter of flat bread, also pushing
the meat toward her.

Michal gingerly lifted a leg of fowl and nipped a tiny bite.
She was amazed that the aroma of the meal tempted her and the
food was savory.

As they ate, the two appraised one another. Michal had
never really looked upon the man before her. She knew his
visage well; indeed she had bathed that very brow. But, as she
was more than the image, she knew this man to be as well. He
had not the splendid beauty of David, nor the dauntless strength.
Mortals did no honor before him as to David.

But Michal had seen in Phaltiel a patient kindness toward
her. She knew of his pain and recognized his great suffering
because of her. He had sacrificed much and was willing to
relinquish all for her. And Michal knew that Jonathan's words
were true. Phaltiel need not have allowed her loyalty to David.

She was suddenly ashamed before the man Phaltiel. She

had ever repaid his kindnesses with coldness and uncaring.

"I wish to thank you," she whispered.

Phaltiel leaned toward her. "Whatever for, My Lady?"

"You have been so good to me."

"And my reward has been great."

"Your reward?"

"To have you in my house. To see you move about these rooms. To hear your voice. These have been reward."

A strange pang knotted her heart and squeezed tears at her eyes. "Phalti..." she faltered as she spoke his name to his face.

Her mind spun wildly. The notion which rose and whirled in it at first frightened her, but as the jumbled thoughts sorted themselves apart, she knew that it must be. She knew that it was her desire.

"I have been bereaved of my husband, David." Michal said softly, looking into his reverent gaze. "If you would have me, I would be your wife."

Phaltiel was instantly upon his knees before her, bowing low. She saw his shoulders shake with emotion. The face he lifted to her was coursing with tears. "I did not believe such happiness would ever come to me. I will cherish you, My Lady, with all my life. I am your humble servant." Phaltiel took her hand and planted a tender kiss upon it and then turned it and kissed her palm.

Long forgotten sensations coursed through her. This was not as it had been with David. She had fallen in love with David. But she had grown into love with the man before her. Unawares, she had found him to be a friend, a protector, a companion. She smiled into Phaltiel's loving eyes, his first smile from her. Michal was once again a wife.

Michal had not seen the house of Phaltiel, before, as she saw it now. It was a grand house, filled with comforts and beauty. The servants, who had grown to love the strange, silent princess who dwelt with them, now joyed in her happiness.

Hogla, ever dear to her, became a friend. They knew that the Master at long last had a wife, for Michal's things were moved to Phaltiel's room. The small chest, however, stayed where it was, and the room was locked.

The blush returned to Michal's cheeks as the flesh returned to the bone. The house of Phaltiel rang with the laughter of the man and his wife, a sound long absent from its rooms. Michal found that Phaltiel's daily absence vexed her, so impatient was she for his return, so that she asked if she may accompany him. With great delight the man escorted his wife through his daily tasks. She, who had only glimpsed the sparser life when in Bethlehem with David, now saw the many men who toiled at her husband's enterprise. She walked among the stalls at market, where she had never before set her foot, and conversed with merchant and peasant patron as well. She was amazed as they bowed before her upon the street. And her admiration for the man Phaltiel grew as each day passed.

"Phalti," she addressed him in her fashion, now, "you have made me happy once again, so I almost forget that I ever sorrowed."

She lay within the crook of his arm. Phaltiel asked quietly, "Do you sorrow, yet, for David?" It was the first mention of David since Michal had become Phaltiel's own.

"I loved him truly, once, and there will always be a void where once that love dwelt. But I don't sorrow." She rolled against him and kissed his beard, tenderly touching the purple scar across his chest. "Your love fills me, Phalti. There is no room for sorrow."

Phaltiel wrapped her in his arms and laid his bearded cheek against hers. "A great void encompassed my whole being," he whispered. "You have filled it, My Lady. Such happiness frightens me."

"Frightens you?"

"Only that it might not last forever."

"It can last as long as we are together. A lifetime."

Death came mercifully to Ahinoam, as she slept. Michal and Phaltiel went to Saul's palace to mourn the queen's passing. Michal did not desire to meet her father, but it could not be avoided. She was ecstatic to see Merab, however, and pulled her aside when opportunity came.

"I see that you will soon have another child!" she said, hugging her sister fervently.

"Of course, Michal. It must always be thus when we meet." They laughed at their joke and strolled into the palace gardens.

"You look so well," Merab observed. "I see a light in your eye that has long been absent."

"Yes," Michal smiled. "Do you remember what you once told me about loving David?"

Merab smiled and nodded with a sigh. "Yes."

Michal suddenly turned, grasping Merab's hands. "I yearned for David so long," she said, "but he is dead to me, now." Her eyes shone and her voice quivered. "I have learned to love Phaltiel."

Merab smiled. "I am happy for you." Her eyes clouded briefly, but the shadows passed and she smiled again.

"Phaltiel is such a kind and gentle man," Michal said fondly. "I have learned to laugh again. I can hardly bear to be apart from him." Michal hugged herself as they strolled on. "It is wonderful to be loved."

"Yes," Merab said wistfully.

The day of their departure from the palace, Michal saw the concubine, Rizpah. She sat upon the balcony playing with her young son. Beneath her colorful veils Michal saw her body bulge. Another bastard to her father's shame!

"I wish never to come here, again," she told Phaltiel as they prepared to leave the city for their home.

"Sad memories of your mother?" he asked.

"Sad memories of my father," she said. "I loved him so dearly as a child."

"You love him still," Phaltiel told her.

"Yes, I suppose I shall always love him," Michal said, a sob catching her voice. "But I despise what he has become, and what he did to my mother."

"Perhaps he was shrewd enough to veil his indiscretions from your mother," Phaltiel suggested kindly. "Perhaps she never knew." Michal smiled gratefully.

Michal received a message from the king once again when his child was born. "His name is Mephibosheth," the note read. Michal touched it instantly to a flame. "The audacity of the man!" she protested to Phaltiel. "He has given to his misbegotten offspring the very name of Jonathan's son, heir to the throne of Israel. What will Jonathan make of it?"

"Your brother will be neither threatened nor tormented by it. Jonathan has a peace within which even your father can't destroy."

"You have judged my brother fairly, Phalti. How can you know him so well?"

"I know enough. I know he is a man who trusts his God, and fears nought but Him. And I know his sister."

The man Laish, the father of Phaltiel, came with great apprehension to visit his son. Michal greeted him as a father. Never a word was spoken of David, and Michal's fondness for Phaltiel was undisguised. Laish went away a happier man, and came to visit more often.

Michal was truly amazed at the lightness of her heart and the easy smile which lingered always near. She stood upon a balcony, wrapped in a shawl against a cool breeze, and lifted her voice to Heaven. "Oh, Lord! How marvelous are Thy ways! I can't understand why I wasn't reunited with David. I can't know Your ways, oh my God, but I trust in You. Thank You for Phaltiel. He is a friend such as I've never known. His love has filled my emptiness, and I've once again found happiness. You have taken the shadows and given me sunshine." She gazed upon the scene before her of bustling city and distant hills.

Suddenly, tears sprang to her eyes and her heart burned within her. "Oh, Lord, keep David in your care! Protect him from my father. His disregard for our marriage bonds has wounded me deeply, but I ask for your protection and care for him. I do not desire him now, for You have given me Phaltiel. But keep him in your way, Oh, Lord."

Michal heard the cadence a of horse's feet against the street and watched a rider sweep from the saddle and run through the courtyard to the door. It was obviously a message of great import which he bore, so Michal hurried to the door.

The man knelt as she approached. Rising at her command, he gave her a scroll. She broke the seal and unrolled the message. Phaltiel's approach behind her saved her from injury as she fell back against him.

"My Lady!" he exclaimed, taking the scroll from her hand. He read the message as he held her. Merab had died in childbirth.

In great sorrow Michal and Phaltiel travelled to Gilgal to lament her passing. Adriel, almost a stranger to his sister in law, greeted them solemnly. In great pomp the king came to mourn his daughter, and Michal avoided him purposely. Jonathan and Neziah accompanied the king, and in Jonathan's company alone could Michal find solace. They spoke tenderly of their sister. Never did a word pass between them of David.

As they departed the tomb of Merab, Adriel fell upon a knee before Michal.

"Rise, Adriel. How can I serve you?"

As he stood, Michal saw a great grief upon his features. "She spoke of you in her last moments, when she knew that she would not live. Michal, you know that I am a soldier in the army of your father. I have five sons," Adriel's voice broke. "I can't care for them. Merab's desire was for you to take them. Will you raise my sons for me?"[56]

The five sons of Merab returned with Phaltiel and Michal to their home, accompanied by nurses and servants. Joel, the eldest of the boys, was tall and thin for his seven years. He herded his younger brothers protectively, and answered for them all. Joshua, aged five, was much shorter than Joel. He was round and jovial, with mischief in his eyes. Almost as tall as he was Jashub, of three years. He clung shyly to his brothers. Adriel was a somber child of two. The infant son of Merab, carefully attended by his nurse, had been given the name of the sovereign, Saul.

The servants of Phaltiel bustled about the big house to make it fit for children. Long abandoned rooms were opened, aired, and scrubbed until they shone. Beds were turned and made with fresh, crisp linens. Yet, the room which Michal had once occupied remained sealed.

Although the boys were given separate rooms, they preferred to sleep together upon one bed, small arms thrown across each other's sleeping forms. Michal, never a mother herself, was suddenly the matron. She soon learned that little care was needed for the physical needs of little boys. But she also learned that great care must be taken for the hearts of little boys.

That first night in their new home, and for many to follow, the poor motherless lads wept and cried for "Mama." Michal and Phaltiel rocked them, cooing tenderly, until at long last the tiny heads slumped in sleep and stiffened limbs relaxed. Phaltiel left each morning exhausted from the night's vigil, and Michal would catch a nap in midmorning.

The four boys moved through the house as one, clasping hands and following the lead of Joel. They kept close to their

---

[56] II Samuel 21:8

nurse and touched their infant sibling at each opportunity, keeping him within sight.

Michal awoke to a bustling distress in the house. She touched Phaltiel's arm lightly. "Phalti, something must be amiss."

As they arose an urgent knock came at their door. Phaltiel met Hogla's wide, frightened eyes. "Master, the boys are gone!"

"The boys?"

"All of them, even the baby. They are nowhere to be found!"

CHAPTER 11

THE PRINCESS AND THE CHILDREN

"Lo, children are an heritage of the LORD: and the fruit of the womb is his reward." Psalm 127:3

Terror gripped Michal's heart. She and Phaltiel walked swiftly through the streets immediately encompassing their home while the servants fanned out into the streets of the city.

"Have you seen four small boys with an infant?" they asked each one they passed. The hours advanced and Michal listened for the hungry cry of Saul. The sun climbed to its zenith. In exhaustion Michal collapsed against a wall. Phaltiel lowered her gently onto a slab of stone and sat beside her.

"We must go outside the city walls and look," Michal said. "How many hours until darkness falls?" she asked.

Phaltiel measured the hour with his eye. "We have many hours." He stood and helped her to her feet. They stopped at a vendor and bought refreshment and then made their way to a meeting point with the servants. Phaltiel instructed them and the search continued.

Michal remembered the twilight of her escape from Phaltiel. Without rescue she would surely have been lost. She could not bear the thought of her five little boys in the hands of thugs. "We must find them, Phalti," she cried.

Leaving four servants to continue scouring the streets of Gallim, Phaltiel and Michal mounted and joined the servants in fanning out from the city gate along the road and through the hillsides.

Fervent fear drove Michal in the search, but as the daylight waned despair overtook her. With tears coursing her face she repeatedly called with a trembling voice, "Joel, Joshua, Jashub, boys!"

Dismounting to search a wooded glen, she and Phaltiel tied their mounts to a tree limb. Suddenly Phaltiel grasped Michal's arms. "Pray, My Lady," he suggested. Michal halted at the abrupt exhortation. "I have heard you pray, often, My Lady," he told her. He shied and looked away from her eyes. "Or do you no longer pray?"

"Phalti." He looked back at her. "I pray. I speak to the Lord each day and thank Him for making me your wife."

Phaltiel smiled. He knelt upon the moss carpet and Michal folded her skirts beneath her to join him in obeisance before the Lord God.

As they knelt thus in prayer a servant of Phaltiel's house approached on foot. "We have found them!" he announced.

The four small boys were huddled in a crevice at the juncture of two walls not far from the home of Phaltiel. The infant Saul slept in Joel's arms unperturbed by flight or hunger. Large, frightened eyes met Michal and Phaltiel as they embraced the children. The sleeping baby was lifted gently from Joel's arms and each boy was carried along the streets to the safety of the house.

Phaltiel and Michal sat upon cushions with the boys while the servants scurried to bring a repast.

"Where were you going?" Phaltiel asked gently.

Joel hugged his brothers to him still. "We were going home."

"Your mother has gone to God," Phaltiel said kindly, "and your father is with the armies of King Saul. You have your own servants and nurse here with you."

Joshua spoke. "But we want to go home."

Michal stroked the flaxen hair back from Joshua's brow. "I once ran away, too, from this house," she told the boys. They turned large eyes upon her, listening. "I ran from here to what I thought I desired. But I learned that what I sought was not to be found. Your Uncle Phaltiel brought me back, here, and now I have learned to be happy here." She smiled at Phaltiel.

136

Joel looked at her thoughtfully. "If we did go home, it wouldn't be the same, would it?"

"That's right," Michal answered gently.

"Father said that our mother desired us to live here with you," Joshua added.

"Yes."

The boys consulted one another with their eyes. "Then we must stay here, with you," Joel told her.

"We want you to be happy, here," Phaltiel said. "This is your home, now."

A wave of recollection swept over Michal at his words. Yes, she and Phaltiel offered a home and love to these boys just as once Phaltiel had offered it to her. She watched their sober little faces and hoped that they would learn to accept this love more quickly than she had.

From that day forth the little sons of Merab became a part of the household. At first they clung together and moved as one through the house. But the love and goodwill of the aunt and uncle who had become their guardians soon eased their childish hearts. Joel and Joshua began to accompany their Uncle Phaltiel to his business, and he returned with tales to amuse Michal after their downy heads were asleep. Although they seemed to accept this as their home, they still slept each night upon one bed, within touch of each other.

Hogla's ancient form revitalized with energy as she oversaw the care of the children. Michal knew that she must go to her bed each night in mighty weariness, yet she seemed extremely content.

The rains began to descend and Joel and Joshua stayed with Michal through the days. Michal gathered the four older boys about her, and holding baby Saul upon her lap, she would unroll the massive scroll of her father and read the stories of the Scriptures. Joel, Joshua, and Jashub joyed to hear their names in the sacred writings. They loved the stories of the men, brave and true, who trusted in the Lord God of the Hebrews.

"Read us Moses, read us Joseph," they would beg, and Michal would comply. Slowly, fairly without notice, Joel, Joshua and Jashub began to recognize the Hebrew characters that told their beloved stories, and soon Michal let them read portions for themselves. Little Adriel wanted to read, too, and Joel would patiently tell him the words to say.

"The Lord is wonderful, isn't He?" Joel commented one afternoon.

"Yes, Joel. The Lord God is marvelous."

"I would like to grow up a be a great man of God like Joseph," Joel said.

"I want to be like Moses," Joshua chimed in. "Frogs and flies and water into blood! I would like to do that."

Michal smiled and hugged her little nephew. "It was God Who did those miracles, Joshua. But it would be good to be like Moses, for he loved and trusted God."

When next Phaltiel went to the high place at Gibeon to the Tabernacle to present his offering to the Lord, they went as a family. Michal opted to walk at Phaltiel's side, accompanied by the servants, who carried the little ones. Adriel would walk and run until tired, and then accept a ride in strong arms. Saul, who was growing to notice everything about him, pointed and jabbered as they travelled. The little boys, who had never before slept in tents, found great pleasure in their accommodations. Phaltiel and Michal found themselves in constant conversation to answer the questions which came freely from the children. The entirety of the feast was exhausting, yet very rewarding to Michal.

As they walked along the road toward home, Joel came to Michal's side. He walked silently for awhile, watching his brothers frolic in the thick grass along the roadside. He seemed to be deep in thought and finally spoke.

"Aunt Michal, my mother once told me that you were married to the criminal, David."

An unexpected pain shot through Michal's heart. "Yes,

I once was."

"But when you were his wife, he was not a criminal, but a great hero of Israel," the boy said.

"Yes."

"Mother said that when he was just a boy he killed a giant with a stone shot from a sling." Joel paused pensively. "He was very brave, wasn't he?"

"Yes, he was brave. But mostly he trusted the Lord."

Joel stopped walking and squinted up into his aunt's face. "Why aren't you David's wife, now?"

Michal knelt beside the boy and grasped his shoulders. She had not spoken of David for many months. She did not know what to say, indeed what she could say. "The King, your grandfather, despises David," she began slowly. "David had to flee for his life from the king. I could not flee with David, and the king gave me to Uncle Phaltiel as his wife."

Joel stared at her for a moment and then nodded his head as if satisfied.

"And, Joel," Michal continued, "I thank the Lord God each day that I am now Phaltiel's wife. I am very happy."

Joel pondered her words and then spoke with a shaky voice. "I thank the Lord God, too, that my brother's and I may live with you and Uncle Phaltiel." He paused. "We are happy, too."

Michal felt confident in her ability to impart to her sister's children the knowledge of the Scriptures, but the king sent a tutor for their education. The boys listened intently as the graying instructor spoke. They carefully copied the Hebrew characters he assigned. He commented to Michal how quick they were to calculate sums. The tutor was clearly astonished at their competence to read. Yet, when the boys gathered around Michal in the evenings they would beg her to tell them the stories of the heroes of their people.

The sounds of laughter and little feet padding across

stone floors stilled suddenly. Michal looked up from her needlework and saw the four children standing in a huddle, little Saul toddling toward them. Silhouetted against the open doorway stood a soldier, ushered in by a servant.

Michal rose quickly and Adriel fell to a knee.

"Rise, Adriel." She herded the boys toward him and coaxed gently, "Your father is here to see you."

The boys advanced timidly. Adriel addressed them awkwardly. A servant arrived bearing a bowl and towel, and Adriel sat silently as his feet were washed.

When the servant had departed Adriel turned to his sons, who stood in a quiet collection, clinging together in silence.

Adriel extended a hand toward them. "Come," he said.

Joel stepped forward cautiously, coaxing his brothers along. Just out of reach of their father the boys stopped. Joel bowed low before him and his brothers followed suit.

"Please," Adriel implored. "Come here." He patted his knee. Slowly, warily, Joel approached, compelling his siblings, until all five boys were within their father's embrace.

Michal quietly left the room, leaving her boys alone with their father.

Adriel partook of the evening meal in Phaltiel's home. Michal watched the strangeness fade between the man and the children. Adriel himself tucked the boys into bed with promises to visit again when able.

Adriel departed before dark had fully fallen, resisting the pleas of Michal to remain for the night. He grasped a hand of each Phaltiel and Michal, and bowing his head before them, thanked them profusely for their care of the boys. "My profession requires that I be gone so far and so long. But I hope to come again, soon."

"Let's take the boys to visit your brother Jonathan," Phaltiel proposed one day. "He's home from the troops just now; I saw him today at the market. Our boys love to play with his son."

Michal smiled inwardly at his words. She knew that Phaltiel loved the five small sons of Adriel as his own.

Jonathan and Neziah welcomed Michal and her large family. The children romped freely with Mephibosheth, who was the same age as Jashub. Little Saul, who could toddle well now, tried to follow the older boys about. Michal had to keep her eye on him closely, for he loved to climb anything that ascended.

When they had finished the noon meal, Jonathan and Phaltiel took the boys to frolic outdoors while Saul napped peacefully. Neziah and Michal sat together and talked of babies and children.

Suddenly, without preface, Neziah asked, "Have you heard about David?"

Michal was suddenly sobered, her mind shifting gears rapidly. She looked at Jonathan's wife and shook her head slightly.

"He is living in the land of the Philistines, in league with the king of Gath."

Michal had no comment for her tidings. Neziah considered her and bit her lip. "Oh, please forgive me, Michal. It was thoughtless of me to mention him." She twisted her hands in her lap uncomfortably. "Jonathan loves David so and tells me each bit of news he gleans of him. Please forgive me."

Michal tried a reassuring smile. "I am no longer David's wife. I am now the wife of Phaltiel."

"Jonathan told me." Neziah paused. "The King has quit his quest for David[57], and of this Jonathan is glad. But Jonathan fears that he may meet David in battle if Israel goes to war against the Philistines again. He could kill David no more than he could kill his own son."

Michal stood and went to a window, resting her arms upon the sill. "The Lord will protect David," she said, "for He

---

[57] I Samuel 27:4

made a great promise to David years ago." She did not look at Neziah. She could not tell her that the Lord had chosen David to be the future king of Israel, for Jonathan was heir to the throne. The chatter of children and patter of little feet freed Michal from the disturbing conversation.

The next evening at home when the boys had been settled into bed, Phaltiel spoke with Michal of the day before. "Your brother loves David."

Michal studied his face. "I know."

"I have married David's wife, yet Jonathan could not keep himself from speaking of David."

"Did he offend you?"

"No." Phaltiel reached to her and held her against him. "I am not offended by Jonathan's love for David. Not as long as you love me." Phaltiel looked into her eyes, his green ones beseeching. "You do love me, don't you, My Lady?"

Michal confirmed her love to Phaltiel.

Michal's life was one of bliss. She was the wife of the man Phaltiel, her nightmare turned to a dream. Her beloved sister had died, but now Michal was a mother of five. Five little hearts clung to hers for comfort and security. This was not her aspiration realized, for that had been a shallow thing in comparison. The Lord God of heaven had endowed her with fullness of blessing, and fullness of heart. Very rarely did the bittersweet memories accost her, and each time she lifted a thankful prayer to heaven.

When next Laish came, he found himself the grandfather of five boys. He had hoped to be progenitor of children of royal birth, but this was not quite what he had planned. The children were indeed descended from the throne of Israel, but not from his family. Yet, the old man's heart was drawn to the five small boys.

Adriel's next visit was brief. Michal sensed in Phaltiel a defensive stance before the father of the boys. Indeed he knew the boys as Adriel had never let himself know them. The boys were polite with Adriel, but Michal knew that Phaltiel was the father of their hearts.

For the sake of the five sons of Merab, Phaltiel insisted upon visiting the King of Israel at the palace on occasion. The king petted each child fondly, and they were happy to see their grandfather. But Michal distanced herself as much as possible from her father. His concubine and her two sons would often be seen about the palace, and Michal refused to acknowledge her or return her greeting.

Upon one visit the king found Michal and Phaltiel upon the veranda. "Michal, my child," Saul crooned. "I have not had a moment with you. Do you mind, Phaltiel?" Phaltiel bowed before his king. He glanced at his wife and exited quickly.

The king took Michal's hand and led her to a couch, seating himself across from her. Without words the two considered each other for a moment. Saul's features, although aged and grayed, were still extremely handsome. His tall frame, however, had begun to stoop ever so slightly. But what Michal noticed most was the dark shadow in her father's eyes, a depth of sadness and despair.

"Michal, my child," Saul cooed, the syllables thick with melancholy. "You loved me when you were young; I know you did. What has happened to us? Why do you avoid my eye, indeed my very presence? Do you despise me so?"

A surge of tenderness swept Michal's heart, but she did not want the dense wall of partition to fall between herself and her father. Could he not know why? He knew. As she looked into his eyes, deep pools of misery, she wondered. Was he trying to ask forgiveness? Was this how his proud heart sought hers in repentance? He had caused her boundless torment. But she loved him still. Never again could she be his little girl, trusting him without question. But always she would love him.

A lump rose to her throat and she fought for words. "What you have done, Father, is what I cannot accept with charity. But my love for you cannot change. No, I despise not you, but your conduct."

Michal saw a deeper shadow veil her father's eyes. "Can we put the past behind us, Daughter?" Saul asked quietly.

So quickly and easily said, Michal thought, but not so easy to do.

"Is there somewhere in your heart a trace of forgiveness for an old man whose God has forsaken him?"

It was a confession. It was a plea for forgiveness. Michal fell at her father's feet in tears, embracing his knees. "Yes," she wept. "There is forgiveness."

War with the Philistines came once more, when the sons of Merab had lived in Phaltiel's house for three years. Phaltiel and Laish were called upon to supply the armies with vestments and victuals, so although the war was good for the economy, the house of Phaltiel saw him little. Fear pervaded the nation of Israel. The fierce warriors of the Philistines bowed to pagan gods, and the army of Israel was led by the hand of God Almighty. Yet all knew that King Saul's heart was hardened against his God. And the great giant slayer was no longer marching with the troops of Israel against the Philistines.

In Phaltiel's absence Michal took the boys to Gibeah to Jonathan's house that she and Neziah might comfort one another. Hogla accompanied them on their visit. Michal's husband was absent only temporarily and not to battle. Neziah's was on the front lines with his father, the king. And Michal knew that Jonathan's dread of meeting David on the battlefield haunted his wife.

The children were playing in the courtyard, attended by their nurses. The servant who brought the scrolled message to Neziah was flushed of face and bowed low before her. Before unrolling the parchment Neziah glanced anxiously toward Michal. She opened and read the missive, blanching at the news. She swooned against the cushions as Michal seized the scroll.

Michal's thoughts whirred and her heart denied as she read the dreadful message. The armies of Israel and the

Philistines had engaged in mortal battle. Slain in combat were King Saul and his sons Jonathan, Malchishua, and Abinadab. Adriel, the father of her boys, had also met his death.

CHAPTER 12

THE PRINCESS SEIZED

*"Have mercy upon me, O LORD, for I am in trouble: mine eye
is consumed with grief, yea, my soul and my belly."*
Psalms 31:9

The news had reached the whole city of Gibeah and fear
drove the inhabitants to flight. When a sovereign was
slain in battle, the royal city was often ravaged, and the
family of the king executed. Phaltiel's servants helped Michal
gather the boys. While the maids of Neziah sought to revive her,
servants brought wagons to the courtyard and swiftly loaded
everyone aboard. In great terror the nurse of Mephibosheth
snatched him up and began to run for the wagons. In her haste
she stumbled at the stairs and she and the boy tumbled to the
bottom. Bruised and hurting, the nurse picked him back up and
hurried to a wagon. Mephibosheth's cries of pain went unnoticed
in the fray.

The gate to the city was blocked with terror stricken
citizens. A muscled servant of Jonathan beat the pedestrians
back with a whip shouting, "Let the king's family pass!"

When at last on the road, the drivers forced the horses to
their limit, until the sweat flew in great foaming clods past the
passengers in the wagons.

Neziah had roused and sat clutching her son to her breast
as he wept. Unwilling to trouble her, Michal leaned forward and
shouted to the driver.

"Where are we going?"

"To Lodebar, to the house of Machir, the father of
Neziah," he shouted back to her.

When Michal was sure that the horses would drop from
exhaustion, she saw the city of Lodebar in the distance, its lamps
glowing through the dusk. The gate was opened to shouted

146

commands and quickly secured after the wagons.

Neziah's family made room for their daughter and her son, and Jonathan's sister with her little brood. When the other children had fallen into merciful sleep, Mephibosheth still whimpered. Neziah held him close but could not comfort him, for her own heart was wounded profoundly. As yet, Michal had not found tears for her father and brothers in the earnest flight from Gibeah. She could not cease ministering to the needs of the others, or she knew the grief would come. Kneeling at the side of her silent sister in law, Michal smoothed the golden locks back from Mephibosheth's face.

"You are alright, now," she told him gently.

"It hurts," the boy sobbed.

"What hurts?"

"My feet hurt where I fell on them."

Michal loosened his sandals and let them fall. She tenderly fingered the feet and ankles and was alarmed to find them both greatly disfigured and swollen. Fetching another lamp she called for Hogla.

Hogla's aged fingers probed the small ankles as she spoke consoling words to Mephibosheth. She ordered compresses and gingerly wrapped both feet.

"His feet are badly broken," she told Michal. "I cannot put them right. He will need a physician."

The long night of terror and anguish finally dawned into day. A physician was sought for the young prince, who said that he did the best that he could. Yet, Mephibosheth's feet remained twisted and deformed.[58]

Michal's boys, young and oblivious to the tragedy, played in the courtyard of Machir. Michal watched their frolic from the shade of a tree. Mephibosheth sat at her side, his injured feet bound and cushioned.

---

[58] II Samuel 4:4

Quietly the boy spoke. "My father will not come back."
Michal's heart lurched. She tried to smile into the little
boy's blue-green eyes. Remembering Phaltiel's words to Joel, she
said, "Your father has gone to God."

Mephibosheth's golden locks bobbed as he nodded. "I
know," he said. "But why?"

Michal knew that she must answer the child, but she had
no answer. Her own heart cried out at the brutality of the truth.
Why Jonathan? She knew her father had tempted death in his
defiance of God. But Jonathan, her darling, her dear brother, had
loved and trusted the Lord. In his wisdom he had been happy to
yield the throne to David, his friend. Why had God taken him?

Mephibosheth's face was lifted still toward her, his
turquoise eyes watching her, waiting.

"Your grandfather and uncles went to God also." Michal
watched Joel and Joshua run past in play. She nodded toward
them. "The father of your cousins also went to God."

Mephibosheth considered her words. "Joel and Joshua
told me that they didn't really know their father. They said they
wish that Uncle Phaltiel were their father."

Michal smiled inwardly. Phaltiel and his boys.

Mephibosheth's sad voice broke into her reverie. "But I
loved my father. I want only him."

Michal fought for an answer to the child at her side.
"They loved their mother dearly," she said softly, "and she went
to be with God."

Mephibosheth turned to watch the boys. "My father will
be happy to see her, won't he?" the child asked.

"Yes," Michal said as a sob rose from her heart. "They
will be happy to see each other." She rose quickly to her feet and
sought solitude. Her heart had been rent, the tears had come,
and she could not restrain the torrent.

On the third day Phaltiel came. Michal thought that she
had wept away all tears, but in his arms she found a fresh
fountain of grief. He held her close, whispering, "My Lady, My

148

Lady," as she wept. When at last she gained control, they
walked in the cool breezes of Machir's garden.

"The Philistines have returned to their cities to celebrate
their victory," Phaltiel told her. "There seems to be no danger in
returning home. We will leave tomorrow."

Michal and Phaltiel offered to Neziah a home with them.
Still dazed at the death of her husband, she could not answer
their offer. Her father, however, answered for her. "Thank you
for your kind offer," he said, "but we will care for Neziah and
Mephibosheth here."

Shortly after Phaltiel and Michal had returned to Gallim
a message came from Abner, Michal's uncle. They were called
to Mahanaim, across the River Jordan, to the coronation of
Ishbosheth, Michal's only living brother. There the tribes of
Israel crowned Ishbosheth as their king.

As Phaltiel and Michal were preparing to leave for their
city, Abner called them to hear a message received from Jabesh-
gilead. The men of that city had taken the bodies of King Saul
and his sons from the walls of Bethshan, where the Philistines
had fastened them. They had burned their bodies and buried their
bones under a tree at Jabesh.[59] When David heard of their deeds,
he had sent to them messengers to bless them for their kindness.
He also challenged them to join him, for the house of Judah had
anointed him king over them. Michal's mind wondered at the
news. David had been told by the Lord that the throne of Israel
would someday be his. Now the kingdom was divided between
the house of Saul and David.

To Michal's great wonder, a message from Jehoaddan had
also been sent with the men of Jabesh-gilead. It was very short
but precious because it was from the hand of her friend. Hastily
scrawled upon parchment were these words:

"David lamented greatly over the death of your father and

---

[59] I Samuel 31:12,13

Jonathan. He ordered the death of the man who claimed responsibility for your father's death. I have copied out a song he sang in lamentation of their deaths."

Michal read David's song, the tears coursing freely, and felt a sweet release from the burden as she grieved with his words.

The beauty of Israel is slain upon thy high places:
How are the mighty fallen!
Tell it not in Gath, publish it not in the streets of
Askelon;
Lest the daughters of the Philistines rejoice,
Lest the daughters of the uncircumcised triumph.
Ye mountains of Gilboa, let there be no dew,
Neither let there be rain, upon you,
Nor fields of offerings:
For there the shield of the mighty is vilely cast away,
the shield of Saul,
As though he had not been anointed with oil.
From the blood of the slain, from the fat of the mighty,
The bow of Jonathan turned not back,
And the sword of Saul returned not empty.
Saul and Jonathan were lovely and pleasant in their
lives,
And in their death they were not divided:
They were swifter than eagles,
They were stronger than lions.
Ye daughters of Israel, weep over Saul,
Who clothed you in scarlet, with other delights,
Who put on ornaments of gold upon your apparel.
How are the mighty fallen in the midst of the battle!
O Jonathan, thou wast slain in thine high places.
I am distressed for thee, my brother Jonathan:
Very pleasant hast thou been unto me:
Thy love to me was wonderful,
Passing the love of women.

How are the mighty fallen,
And the weapons of war perished![60]

Michal sobbed the cleansing tears of memory and sorrow. The truth and tenderness of David's words soothed her wounded heart. Though he had fled her father's wrath for years, David loved him still in his death. David gave to him his due as his king. Her heart had been deeply wounded by David, yet she found there an admiration for the words of the man so hunted, for so long, by the king.

Phaltiel, too, read the words of David. He sat in silence, the open scroll across his lap. Michal saw in his eyes a foreign expression as they sought hers. His red beard quivered when he spoke. "I truly misjudged the man," he said. "I believe that he was faultless before your father."

"The Lord God has at last freed him from his pursuer."

"Have you yet emotions for so grand a soul, My Lady?"

Michal watched her husband's eyes mist ever so slightly. She smiled and kissed the rusty beard. "None," she told him. None, she told herself.

Ishbosheth established his throne in Mahanaim, with Abner as his counsellor and guide. Michal paid due tribute and then distanced herself from the life of the court. Her happy home with Phaltiel and her five boys filled her days and heart.

Michal watched Phaltiel's halting approach from a window. As she hurried to meet him he smiled and reached out to her. Folding her close he whispered into her hair, "My Lady, My Lady!" But when he looked into her eyes his visage was suddenly transformed by concern.

"You are troubled, My Lady," he said softly.

"It is Joshua," she told him, as she watched a smile flit across his lips. Ignoring his reaction, she continued. "Again, today, he led Jashub and Adriel astray. They all were punished,

---

[60] II Samuel 1:19-27

but it was Joshua who inspired the misbehavior. Jashub and Adriel were both duly chagrined at the correction, but Joshua turned immediately to do it again!" Michal fell upon a cushion in exasperation.

Phaltiel sat beside her. He searched for words, then spoke slowly. "I believe our boys are special, My Lady. They will be men of great import. We must learn to channel their energies into worthwhile activities." Michal nodded, agreeing. "They have been schooled sufficiently for awhile," Phaltiel told her. "All the boys shall accompany me each day. They need to learn the business, for it will be theirs someday."

"Phalti," Michal said softly. She put her arms around his neck. "Oh, that it would be the Lord's will to give us a child."

Phaltiel held her close and buried his face in her long brown hair. "We have five boys, My Lady. They are our boys. They are more than I had ever dared to hope for, as are you."

For two years the distinct domains of Israel and Judah ignored each other to the effect of peace. Michal and Phaltiel saw the king only when they travelled to the Tabernacle for the feasts three times yearly. Each time they agreed more strongly that it was the uncle of Ishbosheth, Abner, who held the reins of the kingdom.

Then the peaceful coexistence was shattered. Abner led a contingent of soldiers to the pool of Gibeon to meet Joab and the soldiers of David. The encounter transformed suddenly into a confrontation, concluding with many dead, including Asahel the brother of Joab, the son of Zeruiah, David's sister.

Five years of fierce war ensued between brother and brother as the civil war raged on. Michal's brother retreated in fear and was happy to let Abner rule the troops. Michal and Phaltiel seldom saw the king.

Ishbosheth returned to Gibeah to make ready there for the feast of the new moon. He called Michal and Phaltiel to join him there. They sat to take the feast at the table of Saul, around which had sat great and valiant men. Abner kept the feast with them, and Michal watched her older brother fidget and squirm in the severe presence. When they had at last retired to a veranda Ishbosheth motioned to Michal and whispered hoarsely to her.

"I am very uneasy. Abner is our father's uncle. I fear that he has designs upon the kingdom."

"What makes you suppose so?" Michal whispered back to him.

"He went in to Rizpah, Father's concubine." Ishbosheth lowered his head. "A king's concubines are the property of the heir. Abner has usurped this privilege." Ishbosheth looked again at her and she read fear in his eyes. "When I reprimanded him he was very angry. I fear that he will turn his hand to David."

While Phaltiel joined the men in talk of the war, Michal walked the halls of the palace that had been her home for many years. She wept as she stood in the rooms which she had shared with Merab. She recalled express words spoken and laughter shared. Then the dark memories pressed upon her and she escaped the rooms to the bathing area.

Michal slipped from her sandals and sat upon the edge of the pool, swishing her feet in the cool water. Servants bustled past her and she knew that they readied the room for bathing. Too late she rose to leave, for the concubine Rizpah entered.

The two women considered each other silently. At last Rizpah bowed before Michal wordlessly.

"Rise, Rizpah."

The woman stood and Michal saw lines of care on the face which had been so young and comely. She sought for words to speak to the woman who had been her father's consort.

"Are you and your sons well? Does my brother treat you kindly?"

"We are well." She searched Michal's eyes with large, sad ones. "Princess," she said softly. "Please do not bear me ill."

"You warmed my father's bed when my mother was ill."

"Do you think it was of my choice, Princess?" The question was honest. "I was young, my father was poor, and one cannot oppose the king."

Michal suddenly felt a wave of communion with the woman before her. She, too, had been young and unable to contest the king when she was taken from her husband and given to another man.

"It was neither my choice that Abner came to me." Rizpah's voice broke and her shoulders shook. Michal reached a hand to her.

"I bear you no ill, Rizpah," Michal told her.

Ten years had passed since the children of Merab had come to the home of Phaltiel and Michal. Saul had never known another home. He knew that he had once had a mother named Merab and a father named Adriel, but Phaltiel and Michal were his parents. He was a carefree child, happy to run and play. He loved to spend time with his Uncle Phaltiel, at home and in his business.

Adriel was a pensive child at twelve. He loved to work with his hands to build and with his mind to figure. He could often be found in a corner with the grand scroll of his grandfather, reading the Scriptures.

Jashub at thirteen was beginning to leave his childhood and reach into manhood. He was still a follower of his older brothers, but he would often step out on his own. He grew until he began to tower above his elder brothers.

Joshua, ever the clown, had begun to mellow with the years. At fifteen years he knew what he wanted of life. He worked hard in the business of his uncle, and his stature, although not as tall as Jashub, was muscular and brawny. Yet, for all his size, Joshua would entertain with great gentleness the small children who knew him. With no fear they would crawl about upon him, trusting his love.

Joel, at seventeen, still felt the responsibility for four brothers weigh upon his shoulders. He worked hard at his uncle's side, and was Phaltiel's joy, for he would soon become a partner in the business.

Phaltiel and Michal travelled occasionally to Lodebar to visit Neziah and Mephibosheth. The young prince, still heir to Israel's throne upon reaching adulthood, had never regained the use of his feet. He was carried about by litter, although he could bound around the house of his grandfather upon his crutches. The crippled child played happily with his cousins, hardly acknowledging his handicap.

The family of Phaltiel sat about the table. Animated conversation lit every face and Michal surveyed each with love. Long legs were sprawled over the couches and friendly punches were exchanged. Michal wished that she could hold this moment forever. Her boys were growing up and would someday soon be interested in making homes of their own. But she memorized this moment, for she would want to always remember them thus, laughing and happy around the table.

A servant entered, visibly agitated, and spoke with Phaltiel. He glanced uneasily toward Michal and excused himself. She rose and followed him. Stopping short of the front hall, Michal saw a contingent of soldiers from the palace standing behind Abner, who spoke with her husband. Phaltiel gave a strange cry and his body sagged.

"Ishbosheth!" Michal thought. This could mean only that something had happened to her brother. But she waited quietly.

Phaltiel threw his arms heavenward and wailed. He turned quickly and ran to her, taking her in his arms as he wept. Michal's heart pounded and her mind whirred in confusion. These tears were not for her brother.

"My Lady, My Lady!" Phaltiel wept.

"Please, Phalti, what has distressed you so?"

Phaltiel fell to his knees before her and buried his wet bearded face against her. His body shook with great convulsing sobs.

Two soldiers advanced and reached to lift Phaltiel. Michal reprimanded them scornfully and they fell back. Phaltiel raised his reddened eyes to her and spoke with his sobs.

"They have come to take you from me, My Lady!"

Michal knelt beside her husband and grasped his face in her hands. "Who would take me from you, Phalti?"

"It is an order from the king."

"Ishbosheth would take me from you? Why?"

"David would make a league with your brother. But he requires that first you be returned to him." Phaltiel was again lost to his sobs as he clutched her tightly against him.

"David?" Michal whispered. "No, Phalti, no!"

Soldiers held Phaltiel and Michal's boys at sword point as the servants of Phaltiel hastily packed Michal's things. Michal fell before her uncle's feet, grasping them tightly.

"You are my uncle, my flesh and blood. Please to do not do this!"

Abner answered not a word. He signalled soldiers to pull her free from his feet and turning abruptly marched from the house.

Michal was placed into a litter which was hefted onto strong shoulders, and Abner ordered the column forward. Before they had advanced but a few steps Michal had climbed from the litter and slid to the ground. A shout followed her as she attempted to run back to Phaltiel's house. She was replaced in the litter and secured there with cords. Vainly she tugged at the shackles and cried out in frustrated anguish.

When the soldiers with Abner had vanished from sight Phaltiel and the boys were released. Phaltiel loped in his uneven gait and followed the road quickly after Michal. Joel and Joshua, followed by their younger brothers, passed him up and soon reached the slow moving train.

"Release her!" Joel shouted as he came abreast of Abner. Abner ignored the boy at his side.

Joshua stepped up beside Abner's horse and rammed his stout shoulder against the steed. The animal stumbled, jerking the old general violently in his seat. Abner reached for a whip at his side and lashed Joshua heavily, drawing a deep stripe of blood across his back and arm. The younger brothers stopped in their tracks at the attack, and Joel went to Joshua's aid. Ignoring the searing pain, Joshua trotted after the horseman, shouting.

"Release her! You have no right to take her! She was given to Phaltiel by King Saul!"

"Bind them," Abner ordered the two soldiers riding at his side. The men turned and chased the boys until they had caught and bound each one with strong cords to the trees at the roadside. The sons of Merab screamed helplessly at Abner and his men.

When Phaltiel reached them he passed them without a word, weeping. He forced an awkward run and came close to the column of soldiers. Great sobs of grief shook his body with hopelessness as he stumbled along behind. Almost attaining to Michal's litter he reached out a hand to touch it but was beaten back by the cruel whip.

"Go back!" Abner commanded sternly. "Return to your place."

"You are taking my wife from me!" Phaltiel pleaded.

"She is the wife of David, King of Judah. Go back!"

Phaltiel fell upon his knees in the road and wept. He watched the litter of Michal being carried away until it was but a speck on the horizon. Then he stood and slowly walked back to untie his boys.[61]

Michal heard the shouted exchanges outside her curtained prison. She collapsed in tears. There was no escape.

****

[61] II Samuel 3:15,16

MICHAL, PRINCESS

PART THREE

"I will bless the LORD, who hath given me counsel: my reins also instruct me in the night seasons." Psalm 16:7

CHAPTER 13

THE PRINCESS RECLAIMED

"Deep calleth unto deep at the noise of thy waterspouts: all thy waves and thy billows are gone over me." Psalm 42:7

Michal numbly endured the ride to David's city of Hebron. She heard the pound of horses approaching rapidly as the litter came to an abrupt halt and was lowered to the ground.

The curtain was pulled back. And then Michal saw the face of David. At thirty seven years of age David was still astoundingly beautiful. His beard and curls of burnished brass glinted in the sunlight. His eyes of sapphire took in her condition and he cried out compassionately.

"My Princess! What have they done with you?" He carefully untied the cords which bound her to the litter and lifted her in his strong arms. She lay impassively in his grasp as he carried her to his steed. He stepped up and seated himself with Michal still in his arms. Gathering up the reins he carried her gently into the city to his abode.

When David had shut the door upon them, Michal roused. She stood facing him in defiance.

"Why have you taken me from my husband?" she demanded.

"My Princess," David answered gently, approaching her with arms extended.

Michal took a step backward and David stopped his advance. "I am the wife of Phaltiel of Gallim."

David's face showed a great struggle, and he closed his eyes. They opened with a smile. "Michal," he spoke again softly, "your father had no right to give you to another. You are my first love, my wife, my own."

Michal stood her ground firmly. "If I am your wife, why

didn't you go to Gibeah, while I yet lived there, and take me away with you?"

David lowered his head. "I was a fugitive from your father. The city of Gibeah was heavily armed and guarded..."

Michal interrupted him. "Then why didn't you go to Gallim to release me from the house of Phaltiel and take me with you?"

"I heard that you had become another man's wife," David said, almost whispering.

"I am another man's wife, yet you take me from him, now!" Michal accused.

David lowered himself onto a seat and motioned for Michal to join him, but she stood before him, looking down upon him without expression. They stared thus at one another as the moments passed. Suddenly Michal prostrated herself before him.

"I beg of you, my liege, return me to my husband!"

David rose and walked away to a latticed window. "I am your husband," he said heavily.

Michal went to him and grasped his arm. He turned to look into her pleading gaze. "You have many wives." She paused, watching his handsome face. "I desire to return to Phaltiel."

David took her hands in his and rubbed them softly with his thumbs. His eyes spoke sorrowful volumes before his words. "My Princess, I left you only in flight from your father. I never meant to abandon you. Circumstances were beyond my control. I pity the man Phaltiel, but you are my wife, and I am happy to have you returned to me." David attempted to embrace her, but she pulled free and walked away.

"Phaltiel is an honorable man. He did not touch me, David, when he knew that I was your faithful wife. I would expect nothing less from you." Michal stood firmly, watching the emotions play across his handsome face. "I waited for you, David," she said softly. "I wanted more than anything for you to take me away with you." Her voice broke, but she continued. "I ran away, once, to find you. Then I learned that you had taken more wives to yourself, and I became the wife of Phaltiel indeed." Michal watched tears slide down David's cheeks and run into his beard. "I cannot be your wife, David."

A single sob escaped his throat. He bowed his head and his shoulders shook in silence. When David lifted his face again to her, his blue eyes were wet, but the engaging smile was in place.

"The King of Judah should prove himself no less honorable, my Princess, than the man Phaltiel."

David bowed low before her.

"Thank you," Michal said as he turned and left the room.

Michal fully expected to be taken to the harem to join David's many wives. She was pleased to find that she was given a room to herself. However, the daily routine brought her into contact with the women of David's family. She must eat with them, bathe with them, indeed be in their company often if she left her private room. A servant woman, Perida, was assigned to see to her needs, and her physical comfort was ensured. But her greatest need was in the heart, and the breach there could find no remedy.

Michal recalled the long days and nights spent in grief for David when she was a captive in the home of Phaltiel. Now, confined in David's house no depth of grieving could assuage her shattered soul. Phaltiel! She had truly been one with that man! Her every fiber cried out for him.

And her boys. Surely the grandsons of King Saul would find no welcome in the home of Judah's king. But how could life continue for her if she must forever be separated from them?

On the fourth day of her mourning, Perida announced an envoy bearing possessions brought from Gallim. Michal met him in the courtyard, where David's children played in the sunshine, and a few wives chatted beneath shade trees.

The envoy was her dear heart, Phaltiel. He bowed low before her, unable to restrain his tears. "Phalti," she whispered.

"They do not know, My Lady," he answered, gesturing toward the servants. "I am only an agent, delivering to you your chest." On the ground before him lay the small chest of David.

"Whatever shall we do, Phalti?"

Phaltiel's head remained prone. "Our boys and my servants await the word to attack and carry you away."

"Oh, no," Michal said, dismayed. "They would only be killed by David's men."

"What then, My Lady? We cannot live without you. I cannot bear life without you." Phaltiel raised his tear streaked face and her heart was bruised at the sight.

"Hogla took to her bed when you were taken away. She is deeply grieved that they have taken her dear lady."

"David is King of Judah. He controls great and strong forces. If you could get me away, they would come after us and recover me to David. You would be killed, Phalti. I could not bear that."

"Better to die than to live without you," Phaltiel said.

"No, Phalti."

"We could go to a far country where David's men could not follow us." Phaltiel's green eyes pleaded through his tears. "Nothing is as dear to me as you, My Lady."

"And you, Phalti, are all my heart's desire. But we are powerless against such might. Please, Phalti. Do not discard so recklessly your life nor those of our boys. For me, Phalti, live. Live for our boys. You are all that they have, now. Give them my love, Phalti. Tell Hogla to be strong for them."

A servant approached. "I was ordered to carry the chest to your room," he said. "You are dismissed," he said to Phaltiel. He bent and lifted the chest, then stood waiting for Phaltiel to rise. Phaltiel stood shakily and bowed low at the waist. His eyes locked with Michal's for a fleeting moment of loving communication. Then he turned and walked away, halting greater in his steps than Michal had ever seen. The servant carried the chest away as Michal watched her beloved depart.

The unbearable anguish drove her to her room to surrender to the overwhelming flood of her sorrow.

Days passed, and when Michal could no longer weep, she saw the small chest in a corner of the room. Lifting the long closed latch carefully, she opened it to bittersweet memories. There, among the tightly coiled scrolls penned by the hand of David, was the rough shepherd's garb which had been worn by the young shepherd musician. There was the sling from which had hurled the stone which felled a giant and raised a shepherd to a champion. And there was the small harp which David had lovingly played when he sang songs to his God, the harp which he had played when he sang his song of love to her, the harp which had resounded beneath his fingers as he sang his sorrowful song the night of his escape from Gibeah.

David. She had loved him so in that time of long ago. She had loved him in such pure and innocent faith. But that faith had been shattered. Had it indeed been beyond David's control? Did he in truth care for her yet? Was it love that had compelled him to recover her to himself? Or did he hope to further his cause with Saul's daughter as his wife? Michal remembered a humble David, counting himself unworthy as the son in law of the king. Were his motives good and right? And if they were? Michal had known such love with Phaltiel. Could she once again love David, for whom her heart had died so long ago? Was she still the wife of David?

A great mantle of confusion covered her and buried her beneath its twisted folds. This was a perplexity of sorrow far deeper than she could fathom.

Perida announced a visitor and Jehoaddan entered the room. Michal arose from her seat on the floor beside the chest and with a cry embraced her friend.

"My dear, dear friend!" Michal exclaimed. The two women sat upon cushions and Michal excused her servant.

"It has been so long," Michal said.

"Yes," her friend answered. "Long years, but the Lord

God was so very good to me."

"Are you the wife of Abiathar?"

"Yes. He allowed me a period to mourn the death of my husband, and then we were wed." Jehoaddan paused. Then she said softly, "We have a son. His name is Jonathan."

Michal gasped. "Jonathan. That is a good name." She looked away from Jehoaddan's kind gaze.

"His name is for your brave and valiant brother."

Michal smiled at her friend as a tear slid along her nose. "I look forward to meeting your son."

They were silent for a moment. Then Michal spoke. "Tell me of your life since I last saw you on that fateful night."

Jehoaddan smiled. "We lived in a tent and moved often to avoid the forces which pursued us. Abiathar kept the ephod for David and acted as his priest. And then we moved to the land of the Philistines. The king of Gath was quite fond of David and gave him Ziklag. We lived there a full year and four months." A light chuckle escaped Jehoaddan's lips. "King Achish believed that David and his men were attacking the southern most parts of the kingdom of Israel, but in truth they assaulted the old inhabitants of the land, the Geshurites and Amalekites. Then came the ominous day when David and his men accompanied the king of Gath to battle against Israel. All the men went with David, and shortly after their departure the city of Ziklag was accosted by the Amalekites. Every woman and child was taken captive and the Amalekites took spoil of our homes. We were carried away toward Amalek and on the evening of the third day, as we were camped, David and his men came and fought against the Amalekites until the evening of the next day. Only four hundred young Amalekites escaped on camels. David rescued all the captives and recovered all the stolen possessions."[62]

"But David fought against Israel?" Michal asked. The

---

[62] I Samuel 27,29,30

haunting fear edged her heart. Had David met Jonathan in battle after all?

"No. The lords of the Philistines would not have David and his men fight with them, so Achish sent them home." Jehoaddan looked intently into her eyes. "Michal, I did not know David well when we were young, before he had to escape into the wilderness. But in the years that Abiathar and I have been with him, I have grown to respect his courage and valour. He is a kind man, compassionate to those weaker than he and those in need. His faith in the Lord God never once faltered. I have great admiration for David, as does Abiathar. Wandering in the wilderness and fleeing the troops of the king were small hardship because of the man whom we followed."

Michal was silent following Jehoaddan's lavish praise of David. When she finally spoke it was very quietly. "Jehoaddan, much has transpired for me as well, during these years." A sob caught her voice, but she proceeded. "My faithful slave, Zerah, was executed the day following our attempted flight. My father gave me in marriage to another, Phaltiel of Gallim." The tears coursed down her cheeks, but she pressed on. "He was kind to me and allowed me to be faithful to David. Then I heard that David had remarried, two wives, and my heart died within me. When I recovered from my widowhood I became the wife of Phaltiel indeed. Oh, my friend, I love him dearly! David has taken me from him, but my heart is still possessed of Phaltiel."

"Have you any children?" Jehoaddan asked kindly.

"Phaltiel and I brought up the five sons of Merab and Adriel. They are as dear to me as ever a child of the womb could be."

"My dear friend, I knew that Saul had given you again in marriage to another, but I did not know that you cared for him as you do. I only thought that your restoration to David would answer a long awaited prayer."

"A prayer of long ago, yes." Michal sniffed. "Thank you for sending to me the prayer of David at the deaths of my father and brothers. It sustained me through a difficult time."

"David was truly grieved at their deaths. It was reassurance to his men and their families that his heart had been pure toward the king."

"Do you know David's wives?"

"Ahinoam and Abigail I know well. His recent wives, since he has been King of Judah, I do not."

"Ahinoam and Abigail," Michal asked, "what are they like?"

"They are friends of mine. I love them."

Michal sighed and looked out the window overlooking the abode of David. "What shall I do, Jehoaddan?"

"Do?"

"For fourteen years I was the wife of Phaltiel. Now I have been torn from his arms by David. Can I be David's wife once more? Is it right according to the law of God?"

"Yours is a peculiar case, dear friend. Although you loved your husband, Phaltiel, your father had no right according to the law to give you to another when you were David's wife."

"Could you be happy to share Abiathar with other wives?"

Jehoaddan pondered her question. "What is right, Michal, may not be what is pleasing to you. But you are David's wife. Sometimes one must do what one must whatever the cost to the heart."

"If I am truly David's wife, then what of my years with Phaltiel? Were they years of sin?"

"Yours is a peculiar case," Jehoaddan repeated.

Perida had told her that a great feast was in preparation. Michal answered the knock upon her door to find David, bowing low before her. A swell of nostalgia washed over her as she said to him, "Rise, David."

David rose, smiling. "Michal, My Princess, might I be blessed with the honor of your company at a feast which has been prepared for your Uncle Abner?"

166

Michal was silent for a moment. "Why, David? Why do you want my company? Do you hope to secure favour with Abner because of my presence?"

David's pleasant smile lingered. "No, My Princess. I trust the Lord God of heaven for all security. I only thought that you might enjoy a visit with your kin."

Michal watched the comely face of David. "I believe him," she told herself. "I will be happy to attend the feast," she told him. "I must prepare myself."

"I will wait here, by your door," David told her.

Michal called Perida and was quickly dressed and groomed. A strange emotion filled her as she opened the door to find David leaning against the wall. He stood erect and smiled his illustrious smile again. She let him take her hand, and he led her to the banquet room.

Michal had little opportunity to visit with her uncle. She was on David's left and Abner on his right with Abner's twenty men about the table. But Abner's attention and conversation were directed to David alone. Michal listened as she ate, and the words of her uncle disturbed her greatly.

"I will gather all of Israel to my lord the king, and you shall reign over all of your heart's desire,"[63] Abner told David.

David glanced sideways at Michal. She waited for his response, for her brother Ishbosheth was King of Israel, and her uncle spoke treason against him.

David smiled toward Abner. "I thank you, sir, for your confidence in me, and your offer of aid. However, the Lord told me many years ago that the Kingdom of Israel would one day be mine. I have waited upon the Lord for many years, and I will yet wait upon Him to deliver the kingdom into my hand."

Michal relaxed at David's response and watched her Uncle Abner's countenance fall. "Ishbosheth is no king," he said.

[63] II Samuel 3:21

"The fear that rules him prevents it."

David placed his hand upon Abner's arm. "Promotion comes from the Lord God.[64] Let us wait upon the Lord, my brother."

Abner and his men departed in peace. When they had gone, David invited Michal to a small courtyard to sit in the cool evening air.

"My uncle spoke treason," Michal said.

"And yet, I believe that his heart is for the kingdom of God's people," David answered.

"Thank you that you did not accept his offer."

David's blue eyes looked at her with all seriousness. "I truly meant what I told him. The Lord alone will advance me to the throne of Israel. If I did not believe that with all my heart, I could not have endured the years of flight from your father." Michal could not pull her eyes from his solemn gaze.

Then David smiled and the somber moment had passed. "I thank you, My Princess, for attending me at supper. Are you well? Are you happy?"

"I am well." Michal looked away from him. "Please do not ask me to be happy."

David took her hand and lifted it to his lips. She let it lay limply in his grasp. "I do ask you to be happy. I, too, have faced many difficulties in life. The Lord has patiently taught me to rejoice in Him through them all. I triumphed in the Lord my God even when all hope seemed gone. The Lord gave me the shield of His salvation. His right hand holds me up, and His gentleness has made me great."[65]

David had matured and many events had passed through his life, yet the simple faith that had directed him as a youth was still his stay. His confidence in the Lord God did not waver. A

---

[64] Psalm 75:6,7

[65] Psalm 18:35

memory of admiration for the man before her stirred in Michal's heart.

"My Princess," David said softly. "I would have you to sit with me as queen. Tomorrow I will sit in the gate to attend to the affairs of Judah. I ask that you will join me, there."

Michal was unprepared for David's request. His eyes beckoned as he awaited her answer. "Yes," she said. "I will join you."

The night wrapped them in quietness as they gazed into the other's open soul. David moved and Michal knew that he would kiss her. She struggled with the knowledge, for her heart told her that she was the wife of Phaltiel. Yet, she was the wife of David.

A sudden clamour brought David to attention as his general, Joab, stormed into the courtyard. "What have you done?" Joab demanded, showing small deference for his king. "Why did you send Abner away? Don't you know that he came only to spy on you?"

"Peace, Joab. Abner came only with good intentions."

"The man is the son of a devil!" Joab shouted.

"Joab," David said gently. "You are the son of my sister, and I, too, grieve the death of your brother, Asahel. But Abner slew him in battle.[66] You, my brother, have also slain men in battle, as have I. We are not sons of devils. Abner now offers us his friendship. We must learn trust, again."

Joab turned and strode from David's presence.

David shook his head, sadly. "There is so much hatred. Will we ever leave the hatred behind? I pray that it will be so."

Michal was carefully dressed and groomed in the morning. She was escorted to the gate of the city, where David sat upon a throne. He rose when she approached and seated her at his side upon a similar yet smaller throne.

---

[66] II Samuel 2:23

The citizens of Judah were lined up to bring their complaints before the king. He tirelessly listened and gave judgement. When the line had almost disappeared, a soldier ran to the throne, bowing low before it. His words were garbled with emotion and David patiently waited for him to speak.

"Oh, King! We have found, over there, behind the trees by the gate, the body of Abner, the general of Israel!"

David rose and hurried to the spot. There he fell upon his knees and raised his hands to the sky. He said, "I and my kingdom are guiltless before the LORD for ever from the blood of Abner the son of Ner: Let it rest on the head of Joab, and on all his father's house; and let there not fail from the house of Joab one that has an issue, or that is a leper, or that leans on a staff, or that falls on the sword, or that lacks bread."[67]

After David's strong condemnation of Joab he rose to his feet. "Call Joab to the burial of Abner." He turned to the crowd of onlookers. "Rend your clothes and put on sackcloth, and mourn before Abner."

The body of Abner was washed and wrapped in the clothes of burial. David himself, attired in sackcloth and gray from ashes, followed the bier. At the grave of Abner David lifted his voice and wept, and tears flowed freely about him in the multitude.

"Did Abner die as a fool?" David lamented. "His hands were not bound nor his feet put into fetters. He fell as a man falls before wicked men."

David refused to eat until the sun went down, and the people of Hebron and all Judah understood that it was not by order of the king that Abner had been slain. Indeed, the news of David's lamentation over the death of Abner reached to the Kingdom of Israel and to the throne of Ishbosheth.[68]

---

[67] II Samuel 3:28,29

[68] II Samuel 3:37

When twilight had fallen upon the realm, Michal walked
along a path of stone within the courtyards of David. Upon the
cool evening air drifted a sweet strain. Michal followed it until
she stood beneath a small balcony. Upon the balcony knelt the
monarch, harp in hand, raising a prayer to his God. Michal
stepped into deep shadows and listened to the benediction.

> *Give ear to my prayer, O God;*
> *And hide not thyself from my supplication.*
> *Attend unto me, and hear me:*
> *I mourn in my complaint, and make a noise;*
> *Because of the voice of the enemy,*
> *Because of the oppression of the wicked:*
> *For they cast iniquity upon me, and in wrath they hate*
> *me.*
> *My heart is sore pained within me:*
> *And the terrors of death are fallen upon me.*
> *Fearfulness and trembling are come upon me,*
> *And horror hath overwhelmed me.*
> *And I said, Oh that I had wings like a dove!*
> *For then would I fly away, and be at rest.*
> *Lo, then would I wander far off, and remain in the*
> *wilderness. Selah.*
> *I would hasten my escape from the windy storm and*
> *tempest.*
> *Destroy, O Lord, and divide their tongues:*
> *For I have seen violence and strife in the city.*
> *Day and night they go about it upon the walls thereof:*
> *Mischief also and sorrow are in the midst of it.*
> *Wickedness is in the midst thereof:*
> *Deceit and guile depart not from her streets.*
> *For it was not an enemy that reproached me;*
> *Then I could have borne it:*
> *Neither was it he that hated me that did magnify*
> *himself against me;*
> *Then I would have hid myself from him:*

But it was thou, a man mine equal, my guide,
and mine acquaintance.
We took sweet counsel together,
and walked unto the house of God in company.
Let death seize upon them, and let them go down quick
into hell:
For wickedness is in their dwellings, and among them.
As for me, I will call upon God; and the LORD shall
save me.
Evening, and morning, and at noon, will I pray, and
cry aloud:
And he shall hear my voice.
He hath delivered my soul in peace from the battle that
was against me:
For there were many with me.
God shall hear, and afflict them, even he that abideth
of old. Selah.
Because they have no changes, therefore they fear not
God.
He hath put forth his hands against such as be at
peace with him: he hath broken his covenant.
The words of his mouth were smoother than butter,
but war was in his heart:
His words were softer than oil, yet were they drawn
swords.
Cast thy burden upon the LORD, and he shall sustain
thee:
He shall never suffer the righteous to be moved.
But thou, O God, shalt bring them down into the pit of
destruction:
Bloody and deceitful men shall not live out half their
days; but I will trust in thee.[69]

---

[69] Psalm 55

Tears wet Michal's face as she listened to David's lament of Joab's deed in his requiem for Abner.

Michal enjoyed sitting in the gate at David's side and watching as he judged the citizens of Judah. Three days of the week found him in the gate. David would begin in the cool of the early morning and stay until the business was completed. His people loved him; Michal could easily see that. They accepted his judgement without murmur. The handsome sovereign loved his people in return. He took as great care to settle a minor dispute as to deal with a matter of great import.

Michal sat at David's side, a mere showpiece in the discernment process, for the fifth time. The morning was balmy, with promise of clear skies all day. Michal breathed in the fragrant air which wafted from the blossoms of fruit trees. The hills rose about her cloaked in greens of every shade and hue. Songbirds cocked their heads upon their perches and praised the Maker of the skies.

Michal recalled the words of David. "I do ask you to be happy." Michal could find a peace and serenity in the world she saw about her. She knew a reverent awe for the man who sat at her side effecting caring judgements upon his people. But her heart was still raw with the pain of love torn away from her with no remedy. The place that Phaltiel had forged for himself within her soul could be replaced with nothing else.

A commotion stirred her from her musings as two men were ushered before the king. They bowed low before him. One man bore a bloodied sack in his hand. He pulled the string free and plucked forth a ghastly object. Michal knew instantly that it was a human head, severed cruelly from the body, and she quickly averted her eyes, but not quickly enough. In the fraction of time that she beheld the gruesome exhibit she knew that it was the head of her brother, Ishbosheth. Dark waves of revulsion washed over her senses, chased by anguish. Mercy granted her unconsciousness.

CHAPTER 14

THE PRINCESS, THE QUEEN

"Consider mine affliction, and deliver me: for I do not forget thy law." Psalms 119:153

Michal awoke upon her bed. David knelt at her bedside, softly caressing her cheek. His face was wet with tears.

"My Princess," he said softly. Michal sat up and considered him. Denial had erased the memory, and confusion possessed her. But David's words resurrected the remembrance.

"I am sorrowed that you had to witness such depravity against one of your family." As she remembered, the tears came. But she found her voice and spoke.

"Why, David? Why was Ishbosheth killed?"

"Wicked men slew him and brought to me the evidence, thinking to please me and gain favor. Believe me, My Princess, I was not pleased. I grieve at the death of Ishbosheth. How lamentable for the people of God when a righteous man is slain by wicked men in his own house upon his bed! Those vile persons have been executed for the murder of your brother." David's eyes spoke of his deep remorse. "Will God's people never cease to shed one another's blood?"

Michal touched David's bearded cheek. She wished to thank him for his compassion. What could she say? She found no words. So softly, gently, she brushed her lips against his. She licked the salty tears of David from her lips. Her gesture brought more tears to David's eyes. Tenderly, embracing her gently, he kissed her. It was not a kiss of passion, but one that expressed volumes of unspoken emotions. It told them each that hearts that had once been knit in admiration had not been fully severed. It spoke of trust and respect. It healed in a moment the breach

174

between them, and left them allies against a merciless past.
The head of Ishbosheth was entombed in the sepulchre of
Abner in Hebron.[70]

A sudden distaste for sitting in the gate of Hebron had
fallen upon Michal. Therefore, on the day that the elders of
Israel came to David she was not at his side. But the news was
soon voiced about the home of David. A league had been made
between the elders of Israel and King David, and he had been
anointed king over all Israel.

Soon after his ascent as sovereign of a united Judah and
Israel, David led a company of soldiers to the city of Jerusalem
which was still inhabited by the Jebusites, a Canaanite people
whom the Israelites had never driven from the land. Jerusalem
was situated on the high mountain of Moriah at the juncture of
Judah and Israel, in the tribal land of Benjamin. It was equally
accessible and acceptable to both the north and the south of the
kingdom, and therefore desirable as the capital city of the newly
reunited realm.

The Jebusites, haughty from their long domain in the
midst of Israel, challenged David with scorn, believing him
powerless to overcome their well fortified city. But the Jebusites
were not aware that they dealt with a man who walked and
talked with God, and David took the stronghold, giving to it the
name of Zion, the city of David.[71]

The household of David, as well as those of his six
hundred faithful men, were moved to the mountain top city of
Jerusalem. The houses into which David's wives and their
children were moved were poor by Israelite standards. David
began plans for a palace, and to his great delight he received
messengers from Hiram, King of Tyre, a neighboring monarchy.
Hiram sent to David cedar trees, famed for their value, as well as

[70] II Samuel 4:8-12

[71] II Samuel 5:7

carpenters and masons to work in stone.

The grand palace of David was under construction. He joyed greatly in overseeing its erection. The stone masons and workers with wood relished the visits by the king, and would pause in their labours as he chatted with them. Even the men of Hiram, sent to aid in the building of the palace of David, admired the King of Israel. Each man felt that he had found a friend in the Hebrew monarch.

Michal's room was small and hot, so she found herself in the company of David's harem often, sharing the cool breeze of the courtyard. Cords of sadness struck her heart as she watched David's children run and laugh in play. She closed her eyes and saw in her mind the dear faces of her boys. And Phaltiel! A sob shook her shoulders and she bowed herself upon the couch and wept dismally.

A hand laid gently upon her shoulder brought her tear reddened eyes to David's. A tender expression of concern marked his attractive face, but he did not inquire the cause of her grief. Instead he smiled and petitioned her.

"Michal, My Princess, My Queen. I seek your aid." David pulled her to her feet before him. "As King of God's people I am required to write out a copy of the Law of Moses. I have begun already, but I need a discerning eye to check my copy against the manuscript." David's eyes softened. "Will you help me?" he asked.

Remembrance enveloped her. She saw the dusty archives of Saul and the great volume which she had treasured for years. Yes, David must write a copy; it was the law. Yes, she would help him.

Michal was thankful for the occasion to withdraw from the harem and busy her mind. She carefully compared each character, each jot and tittle, with the ancient copy of Moses. Her eyes tired of the close observation, but her heart thrilled anew to the familiar stories of God's Word.

Some days David had the parchments spread upon tables

176

in a sunny courtyard, or upon a balcony. Other days they bent over David's handiwork beneath many glowing lamps, while the rains pattered accompaniment. Often they would pause in their travail to discuss the people and events of whom they read. David loved the words of God, and in this she and he were in harmony.

Sometimes, when the labour had wearied them both, David would lead Michal away from the manuscripts to a couch. There he would kneel before her, and strumming his small harp, he would sing a prayer to his Lord. Often Michal recognized the words, and at others she marvelled at the new. But always her heart was touched by the music and the songs of David.

Two months had passed and David had not called Michal to aid in his scribal pursuits. She knew that he had been overseeing the building of the palace. She also knew that he had taken more wives in Jerusalem. Perida brought the message to her and she found her way to the sunny porch where David sat, the parchments still rolled before him. He rose when she entered and took her hands. He did not lead her to her seat, but stood towering above her, gazing at her with a curious countenance.

"Walk with me," he said, and lead her down a spiralling stairway. They walked out the gate of David's compound and along a street of Jerusalem.

"I copied out a portion of Scripture which stole my sleep from me," David said as they walked. Michal waited.

"It said, 'When thou art come unto the land which the Lord thy God giveth thee, and shalt possess it, and shalt dwell therein and shalt say, I will set a king over me, like as all the nations that are about me;...Neither shall he multiply wives to himself, that his heart turn not away.'"[72]

David stopped when he had finished quoting and faced her. "My Princess, I have sinned against my Lord." Michal

---

[72] Deuteronomy 17:14,17a

watched the powerful shoulders shake as the mighty King of Israel stooped and knelt upon the street. "I have sinned against my Lord in ignorance," David wept. Michal stood before the anguished king and was unsure what to do. Finally she reached a hand to touch his shoulder. He looked up at her through tear stained eyes and placed his hand upon hers.

"What of my wives? What of my children?" David's body was racked by a sob. "Must I put them away? Must I disavow them, disown my children? I cannot. To commit another wrong will not undo what I have done. I cannot send them away!"

David gazed at Michal as if he needed a word of encouragement from her. Finally a memory floated to her on the still air. "What is right, David, may not be what is pleasing to you. Sometimes one must do what one must whatever the cost to the heart."

David continued to shake in sobs. His blue eyes begged for a different verdict. "I cannot, Michal. I cannot."

David called for two horses. David and Michal rode in silence to Gibeon, accompanied only by two guards. Curious citizens followed at a distance, as their king made his way to the city of the Tabernacle to speak with his friend, Abiathar.

David wept openly before the Lord as he told how his sin had been revealed to him. Abiathar nodded and fetched a scroll. Carefully opening the ancient manuscript he searched until he found the desired Scripture. Then he read aloud, slowly.

"'When a ruler hath sinned, and done somewhat through ignorance against any of the commandments of the Lord his God concerning things which should not be done, and is guilty; or if his sin, wherein he hath sinned, come to his knowledge; he shall bring his offering, a kid of the goats, a male without blemish: And he shall lay his hand upon the head of the goat, and kill it in the place where they kill the burnt offering before the Lord: it is

178

a sin offering.'"[73]

David ordered a goat and knelt in penitent prayer as he waited. When the goat was brought to him, David stood beside the altar of burnt offering and laid his hand upon the goat's head. Michal recalled the day so long ago that she had watched David slay a lamb beside the same altar. With tears flowing freely and great sobs convulsing his body, the king confessed his sin aloud to the Lord. As Michal heard him tell his Lord that he did not know that it had been commanded by God that the ruler should not multiply wives, she believed him. His sorrow was genuine.

David gently stroked the head and back of the small animal, as it jumped and tried to escape his grasp. Then taking the knife proffered by Abiathar David deftly slit the throat in one quick movement. The blood was caught in a basin and David handed it to Abiathar with trembling hands. Abiathar then took the blood of the sin offering with his finger and put it on the horns of the altar and poured the blood at the bottom of the altar of burnt offering. He then cut the fat from the carcass of the goat and burned it all on the altar.

As the smoke of the sacrifice lifted toward heaven David continued to kneel in prayer. When the offering was consumed, Abiathar laid his hand on David's shoulder and said kindly, "An atonement has been made for your sins, my friend. The Lord has forgiven you your sin."

David rose to his feet and embraced the priest. "Thank you, my friend," David told him. Then he turned and walked to Michal. He led her to the horses, where servants held the reins. David helped her mount and they two rode silently back to Jerusalem.

David somberly continued his scribal task. He was nearing completion of his duty when Michal sat at his side, carefully checking the script before her. Her eyes returned and

---

[73] Leviticus 4:22-24

reread the portion before her.

"David," she said quietly. The king looked at her. His eyes still carried the sadness the Scriptures had revealed to him. "Listen to this. You penned it without error. But please listen." Then she began to read.

"'When a man hath taken a wife, and married her, and it come to pass that she find no favour in his eyes, because he had found some uncleanness in her: then let him write her a bill of divorcement, and give it in her hand, and send her out of his house. And when she is departed out of his house, she may go and be another man's wife. And if the latter husband hate her, and write her a bill of divorcement, and giveth it in her hand, and sendeth her out of his house; or if the latter husband die, which took her to be his wife; her former husband, which sent her away, may not take her again to be his wife, after that she is defiled; for that is abomination before the Lord: and thou shalt not cause the land to sin, which the Lord thy God giveth thee for an inheritance."[74]

When Michal had finished reading, David was silent. He had not taken his blue eyes from her face. When he finally spoke his voice was thick with emotion.

"I did not give you a bill of divorce, Michal. You were my wife and your father gave you to another."

"But you took me back from my second husband."

"I did not send you away. That Scripture does not condemn you as my wife."

Michal carefully worded her next statement. "You have the power to give me a writing of divorce. That is my wish. I desire to be free to return to Phaltiel."

David slumped over the parchments before him. "Oh, My Princess!" he cried softly. "I will not do wrong to cover the wrongs already done you. You are my wife. So you shall

---

[74] Deuteronomy 24:1-4

180

remain." Michal felt suddenly stifled in the close room. She turned and fled the room and the man, David.

When his house was completed, David called his people to him for a dedication. Dressed in his richest robes he stood on the stairs before the columned porch. The crowd before him hushed as he lifted his hands. He fell to one knee and slid the small harp from his shoulder. As the peoples of the united kingdom of Israel stood before their king, he raised his voice in a prayer of consecration.

> *I will extol thee, O LORD; for thou hast lifted me up,*
> *And hast not made my foes to rejoice over me.*
> *O LORD my God, I cried unto thee, and thou hast healed me.*
> *O LORD, thou hast brought up my soul from the grave:*
> *Thou hast kept me alive, that I should not go down to the pit.*
> *Sing unto the LORD, O ye saints of his,*
> *And give thanks at the remembrance of his holiness.*
> *For his anger endureth but a moment;*
> *In his favour is life: weeping may endure for a night,*
> *But joy cometh in the morning.*
> *And in my prosperity I said, I shall never be moved.*
> *LORD, by thy favour thou hast made my mountain to stand strong:*
> *Thou didst hide thy face, and I was troubled.*
> *I cried to thee, O LORD; and unto the LORD I made supplication.*
> *What profit is there in my blood, when I go down to the pit?*
> *Shall the dust praise thee? shall it declare thy truth?*
> *Hear, O LORD, and have mercy upon me: LORD, be thou my helper.*
> *Thou hast turned for me my mourning into dancing:*
> *Thou hast put off my sackcloth, and girded me with*

gladness;
To the end that my glory may sing praise to thee,
and not be silent.
O LORD my God, I will give thanks unto thee for
ever.[75]

The godly new King of Israel brought rejoicing to his nation. But when the giant slayer was crowned king, the Philistines marched against Israel. David enquired of the Lord, then led his troops to conquer the Philistines.[76]

As queen, Michal was once again given a room of her own in the new palace, apart from the harem of David. Upon completion of his writing out a copy of the Scriptures, David did not call Michal to him. She passed her days for the most part alone, immersed in thought. Memories of the dear days in Phaltiel's home filled her mind and heart. She recalled the last day with her boys as they sat about the table. She had been happy. They had been happy. And now it seemed so very long ago and far away.

Michal had fulfilled David's need for her as a scribe in his writing of the law. Now she was alone and lonely. Perida was always at hand, but Michal found in her no comradeship.

Through the long secluded hours Michal relived her escape from the palace of Gibeon, so dismally thwarted. She ran on aching feet again in flight from the home of Phaltiel. She had run toward David. Yet, dreaming in the palace of David himself, she rejoiced in the rescue from the thugs by Phaltiel. Each time she let herself remember, Phaltiel was more heroic, more loving, more wonderful.

As the sun began to sink into the west one lonesome day, Michal tossed through her garments in a trunk and there found the hooded cloak. She shook the folds from heavy lengths of

---

[75] Psalm 30

[76] II Samuel 5;17-25

fabric and held the garment to her heart. The back of the cloak was still stiff with the dried blood of Phaltiel, which had never been washed away. Michal licked a finger and ran it across the stain, melting a bit of the time blackened blood onto her finger. She touched the blood to her tongue and fell upon her bed in tears, hugging the cloak to her.

"Phalti!" she cried into the waning light. Suddenly she sat upright and wiped away the tears. She quickly changed her clothes and put her sturdiest sandals onto her feet. With the heavy cloak about her, the hood concealing her face, Michal slithered through the hallways and passages of the palace of David. She reached the kitchen, which was beneath and behind the main palace, and hid behind a huge cauldron. She crouched silently for several minutes, listening. She must escape undetected. She was glad, however, that she had involved no one else in her plot. None else would suffer with her if caught. Tears at the memory of her faithful slave, Zerah, delayed her departure. She dried her eyes and face against the rough cloak. Quietly she crept to the wooden door that led out of the palace to the herb gardens. She opened it very slowly, with only a hint of a creak, and took time to close it behind her as quietly.

Michal hid in a bush just outside the door for several more minutes. Assured that she had not been detected or followed, she quickly traced the path through the garden to the grove beyond. She had only to step up over the foundation of the unfinished wall of David's city. Once past the grove, she hurried her way through the vineyard and out onto the road. She met no travellers in the descending darkness.

Remembering the distant day in which she had fallen prey to thieves, Michal kept a sharp eye on the roadsides, keeping well to the middle. "Phaltiel!" her heart cried, but she tried to keep silent, even quieting her puffing breaths. The sturdy sandals on her feet began to rub blisters as she kept a rapid pace along the road. She was not sure of the distance to Gallim, but she knew that she could not stop to rest until she was safe with Phaltiel.

Michal travelled for hours along the dark, twisting mountainous road. A sudden donkey's bray made her jump and sent her to hide behind a tree. She held her breath and waited. She heard the bray again and stood as still as she could, hugging the tree closely. She stood thus until she felt her knees begin to buckle and her head nodded in sleep against the tree. She could remain there no longer, so she quietly stepped out again onto the road and proceeded cautiously. A snort beside her brought her heart to her throat, and she froze in place. Peering through the darkness Michal saw a small donkey tethered to a tree. Someone must be near. She slid into the cover of the trees and waited again, watching closely.

When sleep threatened to overtake her again, she slowly left the cover of the trees and approached the donkey. Perhaps it would not cooperate and, braying, bring its owner. But she was very tired, and she wondered at finding a donkey there, at such an hour. So she untied the beast and threw her leg over his back. He hunched his back slightly, but did not bray nor balk, and started out along the road at her coaxing. Twice before Michal had fled and had failed to reach her goal. Tonight she must succeed.

"Thank You, Lord, for the donkey," Michal prayed. Suddenly she remembered that she had not consulted the will of God in this flight from the palace of David. She could not pray to the Lord, now, knowing that her deed could not be excused. The small donkey feet plodding against the hard packed earth sang to her ears, over and over, "David will find you. David will find you."

Michal knew that it was true. When David knew that she was nowhere to be found in the palace, he would send soldiers, armed and eager, to bring her back to him. But she did not stop her escape. She did not turn back to Jerusalem.

Pink glowed in the east when Michal neared the city of Gallim. She urged the little donkey to a faster pace as she approached the gate, which had not yet been opened for the day.

Stopping before the gate she called to the gatekeeper, who peered at last out the window.

"It is Michal, wife of Phaltiel," she announced to him. "Open the gate."

The gatekeeper's face blanched and he disappeared. The gate opened just a crack and Michal rode quickly through. Thanking the man, she hurried the little beast along the streets to Phaltiel's home.

Her heart thumped as she slid from the donkey and pounded on the door. She heard voices and saw a lamp light the window upstairs. The door was opened by a servant and Michal pushed past him and into the arms of Phaltiel.

Phaltiel's astonishment held him in confusion for a moment. Then his arms tightened around her and he wept with her. "My Lady! My Lady!"

Phaltiel's lean face had aged and his red beard was streaked with silver. His green eyes were lit with hope and delight.

Michal's bruised and bleeding feet were bathed and anointed with ointment. She was given a cool drink, and the servants fussed over her excitedly. Suddenly she was swallowed in the embraces of her boys. She kissed them and cherished each dear face. They had each changed and she studied the changes. Almost two years had separated her from them, and she could not get enough of their strong handsome forms and their loving faces.

Joel wore a beard. He was no taller than she remembered, but he was stouter, stronger. Joshua loomed like a giant above her. His arms bulged with strength. But his face, framed with his blond hair, had the kindness of a child, and his eyes glowed with love. Jashub was tall and lean, quiet and serene, but animated with joy at seeing his Aunt Michal. Adriel and Saul threw themselves against her, laughing and crying at once. Michal warmed to the love of her boys.

Hogla hobbled from her rooms, her first time on her feet

since Michal's departure. Michal embraced and kissed the old woman. Hogla's form was bent almost double, and her joints moved with great difficulty, but the fire had not burned out in her aged eyes, and they smiled happily.

"Did the king release you?" Joel asked.

Michal smiled at her loved ones, basking in the warmth of their nearness. "No," she said. "I ran away."

Silence fell upon them all. Phaltiel put his arm around her protectively. "They will not take you back," he said.

Suddenly Michal realized the great danger in which she had put these whom she loved better than life.

"Please forgive me!" Michal cried to her family, reaching out to them. "I didn't stop to think of the consequences of my rash act. I only needed so greatly to see you!"

"We have lived as a houseful of dull bachelors without you, Aunt Michal," Joshua told her. "I'm glad you've come home. We'll take care of you."

"Don't fear the king," chimed in Joel. "We'll not let him take you away again!"

"No, please," Michal pleaded. "David's soldiers will come for me, and they will be armed. They will kill you all before going back to the palace in Jerusalem without me." She turned to Phaltiel. "I was wrong to come! Please forgive me!"

Phaltiel held her against him and brushed the moist hair from her brow. "No, My Lady, it was no mistake to come back to us." Phaltiel's green eyes held her as tightly as his arms.

"But I have put you all in danger. I wanted to come back and resume the happy life we knew. But I know it can't be so. David won't let it be so. When my absence is discovered, David will assume I've come here. I love you all so much! Please let me return quickly. It would have been much better if I had been apprehended before I got here. Please, Phalti!"

Phaltiel's eyes filled with tears that spilled over and coursed down his face. "My Lady, life has been unbearable without you. We will all leave together, immediately, and depart the land of Israel. We can make a life together in Egypt, or perhaps north of Mt. Lebanon to Syria, where David can't find us or molest us."

Horses were ordered for the hasty retreat. Before joining Michal and the boys on horseback Phaltiel spoke with a graying servant.

"See to the business," he told the man. "You can manage it as well as I. If we do not return, the house and the business are yours."

Phaltiel mounted his horse. A servant came running, carrying a parcel filled with food and a bag of money. Hurried goodbyes were spoken between servants and family. The sun stabbed the horizon with a brilliant gold as they rode away from the city of Gallim.

Syria was decided upon. Egypt could only be reached by traversing Judah, the abode of David. Michal's weary body swayed with her mount. She removed the cloak and tied it behind her, for the warmth tempted her toward sleep, and she must stay alert.

Everyone talked to her, helping her wakefulness. Phaltiel rode at her side, close enough to reach an arm against a fall. When at last they stopped beneath some trees to take a meal, Michal lay back against the cool mosses and slept. Phaltiel's gentle caress upon her cheek awakened her to the continued journey.

They reached Hamath on the shores of the Sea of Chinnereth by twilight. The inn of Hamath sat atop a rise on the very edge of the sea. The weary family took a room and instantly collapsed on sleeping mats. Phaltiel slept at Michal's side with his arm over her protectively.

In the night a violent wind blew off the sea. It banged the shutters of the one window furiously, and Michal sat bolt upright, crying in alarm. Jashub lit the lamp and Joshua pulled the shutters closed.

"I dreamed that it was David," Michal said in terror,

"come here to take me away from you!" She clung tightly to Phaltiel long after the light had been extinguished and the others slept.

The second day of travel brought hope to Michal. They were now far from Jerusalem and David. Surely David would not know which way to seek her. The servants of Phaltiel's house had not been told of their destination. The day was bright and beautiful, and Michal dared to believe that their bolt would be a success. Phaltiel, ever close at her side, smiled and spoke love to her. They would reach Syria and be free from David. They would have the remainder of their lives together, as they had once before envisioned.

When it came, it took everyone off guard. The boys were chatting and laughing, riding ahead of Michal and Phaltiel, who had relaxed and were not watching the road behind them. The peace was shattered by a loud shout and thud. Phaltiel slumped in his saddle and fell to the road. Michal screamed and leapt from her mount.

Phaltiel lay limply in the midst of the tumult. Michal stood beside him and screamed, "No! Stop! I will return to David! Stop! Stop! Stop!"

The milling horses stilled. Michal fell at Phaltiel's side. "Why did you do this?" she begged of the captain who dismounted at her side. "This is my husband. Phalti," she called softly, cradling his head gently. His blood made a pool around him, and she tried not to see it.

Phaltiel's eyelids fluttered open. "My Lady," he whispered. Michal leaned close to his face. "Death is welcome, if I must lose you again."

"No, Phaltiel!" Michal cried, rocking him gently.

The soldiers all sat their horses watching. Michal's boys crowded around Phaltiel, mindless of kneeling in his blood. As she smoothed the straight black locks back from Phaltiel's forehead, Michal looked up and saw blood coursing from Joshua's head, and Jashub favored a bleeding arm. But the boys cared only for their uncle, whose breath was coming in short gasps.

"Don't try to talk, Uncle Phaltiel," Joel said comfortingly. "We will get you back to Hamath and call a physician."

Tears were flowing with the blood down Joshua's face. "You'll be alright," he wept.

"You must come with us," the captain told Michal uncertainly.

She glared at him through her tears. "You wounded my husband. I will take him to Hamath and see that he is cared for." She withdrew her gaze from him and said quietly, "Then I will return with you to Jerusalem."

Phaltiel sighed sharply, drawing all attention back to his drawn face. He lifted a bloody hand to Michal's face and drew her close once more. "I'm so pleased that you came back," Phaltiel murmured. A violent cough racked his body. Very weakly he whispered, "To see you one more time has made me so happy." Phaltiel shuddered and went limp against Michal. His emerald eyes, no longer shining, stared into the bright blue sky.

Michal hugged the lifeless body of Phaltiel to her and continued the slow rocking. Her grief was deeper than words. Her boys wept with her.

"Uncle Phaltiel," Adriel called.

"Uncle Phaltiel has gone to God," Joel told him gently.

The soldiers would not allow Michal to accompany the body of Phaltiel back to Gallim. She hugged her boys and sadly watched them leading Phaltiel's horse back toward their home. Her deep loss made her heart heavy. Phaltiel had died because of her thoughtless flight from David. As she rode beside the soldiers toward Jerusalem, she pondered plunging from her horse into a deep abyss beside which they passed. She cared no more for life. Always at the palace of David she could remember Phaltiel and dream of being with him again. Now only death could reunite them.

CHAPTER 15

THE PRINCESS DISPOSSESSED

"For in the time of trouble he shall hide me in his pavilion: in the secret of his tabernacle shall he hide me; he shall set me up upon a rock." Psalm 27:5

Michal returned to a Jerusalem that was thrumming with excitement. David had called all the congregation of Israel to him to Jerusalem, the captains of thousands and captains of hundreds, and all the priests and Levites. The ark of the covenant, the symbol of the very presence of the Lord God with His people, was in Kirjath-jearim, in the house of Abinadab. Many years ago, before the Lord had given Israel their first king, Saul, the ark of God had been taken by the Philistines. Great troubles came to them because of the ark, and it was returned to the city of Kirjath-jearim, to the house of Abinadab. There his son, Eleazar, was set apart to keep the ark.[77]

King David, whose heart was always tender toward the Lord God, had a great desire to carry the ark to Jerusalem. It had been neglected and ignored during the reign of Saul. The ark of the covenant was the symbol of the very presence of God, and David desired to have it near, to enquire of God before it.

Michal grieved alone in Phaltiel's death. Even Perida was caught in the exhilaration of David's plans. A grand assembly of musicians was gathered with harps and psalteries, timbrels, cymbals and trumpets. David lead a great choir in praises to the Lord. A new cart was artfully crafted and intricately carved.

The day dawned upon an elated multitude gathered to fetch the ark to Jerusalem. David himself lead the procession from the royal city to Kirjath-jearim. Eleazar the son of

---

[77] I Samuel 7:2

Abinadab, now gray with age, delivered the ark to David with tears of joy. Two men, Ahio and Uzza, were chosen to drive the cart bearing the ark to the city of David. David and the musicians played before the ark loudly. The choir was joined by the thronging masses and the singing rose heavenward with exultation.

As the grand parade came to the threshing floor of Nachon, the oxen shook the cart. Uzza took hold of the ark to steady it. Suddenly he shrieked and fell from the cart to the ground. Those near the cart panicked and tried to escape. In a moment the joyous company was transformed to confusion and fear.

David ran to the cart and fell on his face before the Lord. Fear filled his heart at Uzza's death. "How will I take the ark of the Lord to Jerusalem?" he cried.

At the edge of the road, bordering Nachon's threshing floor, was the house of Obed-edom, a Gittite. The cart was carefully driven to the door. Obed-edom ran from the throng and fell before the king.

"I am afraid of what the Lord has done," David told him. "I can't carry the ark to Jerusalem. Will you keep it here, in your house, for me?"[78] David did not demand, but his blue eyes pierced any objection from Obed-edom.

"It is my delight, Sire," he said.

David and the great multitude returned to Jerusalem sorrowfully.

Sitting at her window in a black gown of mourning, Michal tried to think of nothing, but again her mind saw Phaltiel's green eyes in death as he lay in a pool of blood. A deep emptiness suffocated her and she had no will to live.

Perida, who had chatted so gaily in the morning, entered the room with shadows. Michal felt the change in her and saw

[78] II Samuel 6:1-10

that her eyes were red and swollen.

"Why do you weep?" Michal asked.

Perida fell before her. "My queen, I know that you are unaware in your deep grief."

"Unaware of what, Perida?"

"The Lord struck the driver of the cart dead, and my lord the king is in desperation to bring the ark to Jerusalem."

Michal had no sympathy for David's despair. He had brought such suffering to her, now, that she could never again care for him.

The days that followed were the darkest Michal had ever known. Her days of mourning in the home of Phaltiel had been festive in comparison. Michal grew gaunt and listless.

"My queen," Perida announced. "A visitor to see you. The lady Jehoaddan."

Michal was instantly on her feet and in the arms of her friend. She wept against Jehoaddan and her friend embraced her, patting her back in comfort.

When at last they were seated, Michal grasped Jehoaddan's hands in hers. "Phaltiel was so good to me," Michal said. "I loved him with all my heart and soul." She looked viciously into her friend's eyes. "David killed him."

Jehoaddan's face was lined with coming age. Her hair was streaked with gray beneath her hair covering. She smiled kindly and said, "Michal, my friend, I sorrow with you at your bereavement. I never knew Phaltiel, but I do believe that he was good to you. Please don't blame David. He is your husband. He only feared for your safety. It was not his desire that anyone should be injured. It was not his will that Phaltiel die."

Michal wiped away the tears that blurred her vision. "David does not even care that Phaltiel is dead. He has not spoken to me at all. I doubt that he even cares that I have been returned to him."

Jehoaddan stroked Michal's hands with her thumbs. She spoke softly. "David has been grievously disappointed. He

192

wanted so to bring the ark to Jerusalem. His intentions were all good. He loves the Lord so. The death of Uzza lies heavy on his heart. He can't understand why God struck him dead, when David's purpose was so pure. It is true, dear friend, he may not be aware of the awful fate which befell you. Perhaps he has not even been told."

"Jehoaddan, what am I to do?" Michal suddenly cried. "Phaltiel is gone and my heart with him. David has no desire nor need for me. I am trapped here, in David's palace. I can't be with my boys. Life means nothing to me, now."

Jehoaddan spoke softly. "In thee, O Lord, do I put my trust; let me never be ashamed: deliver me in thy righteousness. Bow down thine ear to me; deliver me speedily: be thou my strong rock, for an house of defence to save me. For thou art my rock and my fortress; therefore for thy name's sake lead me, and guide me."[79]

The gentle words soothed Michal's heart. "David?" she asked quietly.

"Yes. David penned them, Michal, but the words are the Lord's. Although all else fails, the Lord God is ever near. He will not desert you. Trust in Him."

Michal looked into her friend's compassionate eyes. "I haven't prayed since Phaltiel's death." She looked away. "Indeed, I didn't pray before I ran away to him. I feared to ask God's will. I supposed it would not be to go to Phaltiel. So I didn't pray. Look what I've done!" Michal threw herself back into Jehoaddan's embrace. "If I had not gone to him, he would still live."

Jehoaddan patiently soothed her. "You are not at fault. You only followed the leading of your heart. But now you must go on. You must pray. You must trust in God, Michal."

They could not chat as they had done when girls in the

---

[79] Psalm 31:1-3

193

city of Nob. Life had dealt each too many blows of sorrow. But the two women who sat in the palace of David drew strength and hope from one another as they sat late into the twilight, talking as only friends can.

Michal followed Jehoaddan's counsel. She tried to pray. But she could not find words to speak the deep void within her. She ordered the great scroll of Saul brought to her, and found her heart calmed by the reading of the familiar words. Finding comfort in the Scriptures, Michal read them every waking moment. She read of God's care for His people, but in the fifth book of Moses she found words that soothed her hurting heart. "Yea, he loved the people; all his saints are in thy hand: and they sat down at thy feet; every one shall receive of thy words."[80]

Michal closed her eyes and let the tears squeeze through and slip along her nose. "O God," she prayed. "do you love me?" She waited, as for an answer. "Am I in Your hand?" she continued to pray. "I desire to sit down at Your feet. I want to receive of Your words. I need You. Phaltiel has gone to You. I cannot find comfort in David. His heart and time are taken with so many other things. Help me, O Lord!"

Michal opened her eyes and watched the sunlight filter through a latticed window. No audible words came to her ears, but the small still voice of God spoke to her heart and eased her pain at last.

At reaching the end of Moses' writings, Michal began again, reading of the creation of the heaven and the earth. She read the stories of the patriarchs of Israel and of Moses leading God's people out of bondage in Egypt. Then, as she read God's instructions to Moses for the construction of the Tabernacle, she read, "And thou shalt put the staves into the rings by the sides of the ark, that the ark may be borne with them."[81]

---

[80] Deuteronomy 33:3

[81] Exodus 25:14

"David," Michal whispered. She thought of the continual torment the king knew. "David needs to know this," she told herself. But she did not go to him. She remained in her room, reading the Scriptures.

When Michal again reached the fifth book of Moses, she read, "At that time the Lord separated the tribe of Levi, to bear the ark of the covenant of the Lord, to stand before the Lord to minister unto him, and to bless in his name, unto this day."[82]

Michal leaned back against the cushion of her seat and stared at the ceiling of her palace room. She must tell David. From God's word she had the answer to his troubles. She must share it with him. Through His word the Lord had consoled her grief. Did she desire that David should continue to suffer because of the pain he had caused her?

Michal bowed before the Lord. "My God," she prayed. "David has repeatedly brought me anguish. Why should I show him this?" The answer came, not to her ears but to her heart.

Michal was ushered into David's presence. She stood before him quietly, observing his graying head bent low in prayer. When he lifted his head deep sadness lay in his sapphire eyes. He smiled and stood to his feet, extending a hand to her.

"My Queen! Come, sit." David led her to a seat beside his and continued to hold her hand. He gazed at her quietly for several moments, his expression taking on great concern as he noted her gaunt features. "Are you ill?"

"Sick at heart, my king," Michal said.

David continued to gaze at her, sorting his thoughts in silence. "The man Phaltiel," he said simply.

"Yes. He was killed by your men." Michal looked into his blue eyes fervently. "I would have gone with your men of my own will. There was no need to kill..." Michal's voice broke and she collapsed into tears. David moved to embrace her, but she

---

[82] Deuteronomy 10:8

pulled away. "My heart died with Phaltiel!" she said, rising to her feet. She walked away from him. He rose and followed her.

Michal turned and faced David. He stood before her in his melancholy beauty, the shepherd musician, the warrior, the King of Israel. At that moment she wished to dissolve away the years that had elapsed and be his princess once again, his one and only love. But she shook the emotion from her.

"I have come to tell you what I have read in the Scriptures."

David raised his eyebrows and nodded.

"The Lord God commanded that the ark of the covenant be borne by Levites with the staves upon their shoulders," she told him.

David was silent for a moment, assimilating the information. Then, suddenly, he grasped Michal and hugged her to him. "That's it! We didn't do it God's way. Thank you, My Princess!" David kissed her cheek and released her. Although eager to act upon her testimony, he paused, seeking her eyes.

"Can you find it in your heart to forgive me? I sorrow with you in your bereavement." He knelt before her, head bent low. Michal recalled a time so long ago when another monarch had asked her pardon. Could she forgive the man who had caused Phaltiel's death? She didn't know. Without answering him she left the room, leaving the king kneeling upon the floor.

David led the rejoicing throng of Israel to the home of Obed-edom. With great singing and music, accompanied by soldiers on horseback and on foot, the multitude followed the four Levites who bore the ark upon their shoulders. When they had advanced six paces, David stopped the procession. There an altar was built and seven oxen and seven rams were offered to the Lord in thanksgiving for His grace. Then, David leading the train, they continued on to Jerusalem with great joy.

David was clothed in a fine linen robe and the ephod of a priest. In celebration of the safe conveyance of the ark to Jerusalem, he danced before the Lord with all his might.

Michal stood at a window of David's palace and watched the parade enter the city and wend its way toward the tent that David had prepared for the ark. The jubilant crowd, the clamour of song and musical instrument, and the frenzied dance of David overwhelmed her and she was swept with repulsion. Disgusted, she turned from the scene. No, she could find no forgiveness for him in her heart.

The festivities of the day extended into the twilight. Sacrifices were offered before the ark by the priests ordained by David. The family of Obed-edom were appointed porters of the tabernacle in which the ark was placed. A loaf of bread, a piece of meat, and a flagon of wine were given to each man and woman, and finally the great multitude turned homeward.

Michal saw David returning to his home, and she went to meet him.

"How glorious the King of Israel was today!" she greeted him in scorn. "The king, who uncovered himself today in the eyes of the handmaids and servants, like an arrogant fool uncovers himself without shame!"

David, still jubilant from the great day of rejoicing, sobered suddenly. "I danced before the Lord, Who chose me before your father, and before all your family, and appointed me the ruler over Israel, the people of the Lord." David spoke slowly, deliberately. "I will play before the Lord, and I'll be base in my own sight. And I'll be honoured in the sight of the maidservants you spoke about."

Michal felt only contempt for the man before her. She held her head high. Turning from him she walked away.

Only the visits from Jehoaddan brought any light into Michal's dark existence. But even Jehoaddan could not lift her spirits from her deep loneliness.

As King of Israel, David was a great success. He led the armies of Israel against the Philistines one last time and defeated them. In battles against Syria he extended the kingdom to the River Euphrates. His people loved him. The heathen nations ordering his realm respected him. His God blessed him.

As David fought for the Lord, Michal's personal battle continued. The love that had once ruled her heart now burned as hatred toward David. But for the Scriptures to which she often turned for comfort, Michal would have languished away.

A soft breeze greeted Michal and Jehoaddan as they walked among the trees of the palace garden. Jehoaddan's happiness at the appointment of her son as a priest before the ark of the covenant brought a smile to Michal's lips, her first in weeks.

Jehoaddan sighed. "The priests and Levites all seek the face of God about the drought," she said. "Thus far no answer has been given. Abiathar said that Jerusalem is secure for some time, but many of the cities and villages have small stores of food, since the rains were scarce last year as well. They depend greatly on the yearly harvest. Why the Lord is withholding the rains cannot be determined. The ark of God has come to rest in Jerusalem. Our king leads us in the way of the Lord." She sighed again, shaking her head.

Suddenly, Jehoaddan laid her hand on Michal's arm and they stopped walking. "Have you heard that David is seeking the son of Jonathan?"

"Mephibosheth!" Michal cried. "Why would David seek him?"

"I don't know."

Michal's heart constricted. She knew that sovereigns often destroyed all competition by killing the family of the former king. Mephibosheth had been heir to Saul's throne. She clutched Jehoaddan fearfully. "Mephibosheth is no threat to David. What could he want with him?"

"I'm sure David intends him no harm," Jehoaddan said softly.

Michal was not consoled. She no longer knew David. She must stop him, whatever his design.

CHAPTER 16

THE PRINCESS AND THE PRINCE

"Hide not thy face far from me: put not thy servant away in anger: thou hast been my help; leave me not, neither forsake me, O God of my salvation." Psalm 27:9

Michal strode with purpose to David's council room. The guard at the door attempted to impede her, but she gave him a withering glance and entered the room. David sat at a small table engaged in conversation with a man who sat across from him. He looked up when Michal entered.

"My Princess!" David rose and met her. She did not take his proffered hand. The caller rose also, and Michal recognized the steward of her father's lands. Ziba was aged and grayed, but she knew him at once.

"Why do you seek Mephibosheth?" Michal demanded of David.

A broad smile lit David's face, smoothing away the years and stinging Michal's heart with memories of the shepherd boy she had loved. "The son of Jonathan." David spoke the name of her brother in gentle reverence. David's blue eyes misted. "I loved Jonathan better than life." David's eyes closed and a tear slid free. "Oh that he had lived to see the blessings of the Lord upon His people!"

David swallowed and opened his eyes. His dazzling smile returned, and he gestured toward the servant. "Ziba, the steward of King Saul's lands has told me that Jonathan's son still lives. I'll bring him here, My Princess, and I'll show him kindness for Jonathan's sake."

Michal watched the face of David. Yes, she believed that his motive was blameless. David wanted only to share with Mephibosheth a portion of the love he had held for Jonathan.

"Jonathan would be happy," Michal said simply. She

turned and left the room.

The arrival of Mephibosheth to Jerusalem was a grand occasion. Many lived in the tribe of Benjamin and in Jerusalem itself who had honoured King Saul and loved his handsome son, Jonathan. But none, least of all Michal, was prepared for the spectacle which met their eyes as the son of Jonathan rode regally into the city of Jerusalem upon a white steed. At twenty-one years, Mephibosheth's blonde beauty was a reflection of Jonathan. His golden hair and beard, his handsome face, and his princely bearing all mimicked Jonathan.

The citizens thronged close about his horse, reaching to touch him, marvelling at the likeness. When a soldier raised a whip to drive them away, Mephibosheth prevented him, allowing the coursing multitude to slow his progress. He smiled and greeted the people who paid him homage, and Michal's heart broke with the dear memories of Jonathan.

Inside the palace walls, with only his attendants and the inhabitants of the palace to witness, Mephibosheth was lifted from the horse and given his crutches. David ran to him, and for a moment, Michal believed that David would fall prostrate before Jonathan's son. But Mephibosheth dropped his crutches and fell on his face before his king.

"Mephibosheth!" David said with great compassion.

"I am your servant, sire."

David lifted the crutches and helped Mephibosheth onto his feet. "Don't be afraid. I'll show kindness to you for your father Jonathan's sake. I'll restore all the land of your father, Saul, to you, but you'll eat bread at my table as one of my sons."

Clutching the crutches, Mephibosheth bowed himself and said, "Who am I, that you should look upon such a dead dog as I am?"[83]

David could restrain himself no longer but embraced the

---

[83] II Samuel 9:8

young man with tears. "Your father and I loved one another dearly. We pledged to each other to care for one another's children. I will do for you, Mephibosheth, as though it were for Jonathan."

From a litter stepped a young woman with an infant in her arms. Mephibosheth beckoned her and presented her to David. "This is my wife, Adah, and my son, Micha."

Mephibosheth's family were given rooms in the palace, and they lived of the fare of the king. Ziba and his sons, with many servants, were given the care of Saul's lands, now Mephibosheth's. The fruits of the lands were to belong to Mephibosheth.

When the excitement had quieted, Michal made her way to the apartment of Mephibosheth and Adah. The servants melted away as she sat with them upon cushions.

"I am so sorry about Uncle Phaltiel," Mephibosheth told her. "But I am happy that you are here, in the palace, and we shall see you often."

Michal held the baby Micha in her arms, rocking him gently. "Do you see my boys now and then?"

"Yes. We have visited them, and they us. Joel, Joshua, and Jashub carry on the business of Phaltiel, and quite well, too. Joel has taken a wife..."

Michal gasped, and then began to weep softly, as Mephibosheth continued.

"Joshua is betrothed and will wed soon. Jashub has his eye on a maiden, and hopes to have the dowry as soon as possible. Adriel has become quite a scribe, and hopes to find a position in that calling. Saul waits for his age so that he may be a soldier, as his father was."

For several moments Michal wept for the boys she loved. How she wished to share their lives!

When composed, she asked, "Your mother, how is she?"

Mephibosheth's aqua eyes told her before he spoke. "My mother died of a broken heart two years ago."

"What of Hogla?"

"She went soon after..."

"Phaltiel," Michal finished.

"Yes."

They were silent for awhile, listening to the deep breathing of the sleeping infant. Then Michal smiled at Mephibosheth and his wife. "I'm so glad you've come!"

With Mephibosheth's family in the palace Michal found a new purpose. She could not share in the lives of the wives and children of her boys, but she could in Mephibosheth's. She grew to love the young woman Mephibosheth had married, and she adored his little son.

The occupants of the palace of King David would hardly have known that a famine existed but for visitors to the throne. Fields lay dormant although planted, the seeds decaying in the dry soil without rain. The fig, pomegranate, and olive trees, as well as the grapevines leafed sparsely, and bore very little fruit. The grasses which fed the cattle and sheep withered and browned beneath the scorching sun. Not even a cloud drifted across the skies to cast a shadow of relief.

A steady stream of complainers made its way before the throne of David. He prayed and begged for the reason for the famine. He tried in vain to comfort his subjects, who feared for their families. He wept when his people returned to their hungry homes, prostrating himself before the Lord for an answer.

In the midst of his troubles, David learned that Nahash, the king of the neighboring nation of Ammon, had died. His son, Hanun, reigned in his place. Nahash had shown kindness to David when he fled from Saul so many years in the wilderness, so David sent servants to Hanun to express his sympathy at the death of his father.

Few were aware of David's show of benevolence, nor did they care. A meager harvest was being severely rationed, and hunger was the utmost concern of Israel's people. But their attention was drawn to Ammon, when the messengers of David

202

sent to him from the city of Jericho. David sent envoys to meet them there, and found that Hanun had disgraced the men by shaving off half of their beards and cutting off their garments to their buttocks. David was distressed that his message of kindness had been brutally rejected. But then he heard that the nation of Ammon and hired troops from Syria were marching against Israel.

Joab led the troops of Israel against the Ammonites and Syrians. The attention of the kingdom was diverted from the hunger, waiting fearfully for the soldiers to return. At last Joab returned, followed by the weary men of Israel and Judah. A victory had not been secured, but the armies of Ammon and Syria had fled before the armies of the Lord.

Everyone supposed the trouble had ended until word came to David that the Syrians had regrouped and were joined by reinforcements. They marched toward Helam, across the Jordan River.

This time David himself lead the armies of Israel. Michal believed him to have already departed when they met in the palace courtyard. He wore the garb of a soldier, covered by a large cape. His eyes betrayed his smile as he greeted her. She murmured a greeting and would have passed by him, but he reached a hand to stop her.

"My Princess," he said, a tremor in his voice. "I have petitioned the Lord for the cause of the drought, but He has not responded. I must face the armies of Syria, and I cannot go in my own feebleness. Always I have faced the enemies of the Lord our God with assurance in my heart that He led His armies and that victory was secure. I have prayed that the Lord will forgive my doubts. He is the same as He ever has been." David seemed reassured by his own words to her. The concern melted from his eyes. "Will you pray, My Princess, for victory for the Lord's army?"

"I will, my lord."

As Michal walked away from David she heard him softly

strumming his harp. He raised a prayer in song to his God.

They that trust in the LORD shall be as mount Zion,
Which cannot be removed, but abideth forever.
As the mountains are round about Jerusalem,
So the Lord is round about his people from henceforth
even for ever.
For the rod of the wicked shall not rest upon the lot of
the righteous;
Lest the righteous put forth their hands unto iniquity.
Do good, O LORD, unto those that be good,
And to them that are upright in their hearts.
As for such as turn aside unto their crooked ways,
The LORD shall lead them forth with the workers of
iniquity: but peace shall be upon Israel.[84]

David returned triumphantly with his men from the battle with Syria. The Lord God had given victory to His armies and the Syrians made peace with Israel and conceded to serve David.

Michal had no more encounters with David upon his return. Their lives, although lived within the same walls, were altogether separate. Michal spent much time with Mephibosheth and Adah, but never accompanied them to David's table, preferring to take meals alone.

Jehoaddan visited often, always filled with news to cheer Michal, and eager to hear about Mephibosheth's family. As the days and weeks of drought dragged on, Jehoaddan brought cheerless reports that the priests of God had not yet determined the cause.

The third year of drought brought severe hunger and suffering as the time of barley harvest came with no yield from the ground.

Jehoaddan came one afternoon accompanied by a woman veiled in black. As they entered the room, the woman ran to

---

[84] Psalm 125

Michal and prostrated herself at Michal's feet.

"Help me, Queen Michal," she wailed.

Together Jehoaddan and Michal lifted the woman and seated her in a chair.

"She came to me pleading to be brought to you," Jehoaddan explained.

Michal pulled the veil from the woman's face and gasped. It was her father's concubine, Rizpah. Her eyes were red and puffy from weeping, and her graying hair clung in strings about her face. She threw herself upon the floor again before Michal and moaned.

"Please help me!"

Michal and Jehoaddan lifted Rizpah to her seat once more.

"How can I help you, Rizpah?" Michal asked gently. "What is it that you want of me?"

"The king will give them my sons!" she cried, beginning to tremble uncontrollably.

"Give your sons to whom?" Michal asked, trying to comprehend the woman's grief.

"To the Gibeonites! They will hang them! Please help me! You can speak to the king. I beg of you, help me!"

Rizpah collapsed into convulsive sobs. Michal looked at Jehoaddan for an answer, but she had none. The two women tried to console her enough to learn more, but she blubbered helplessly, and could offer no more information.

"Take care of her," Michal said to Jehoaddan. "I will enquire of David." She patted Rizpah's shoulder. "I will try, Rizpah."

Michal couldn't find David. He wasn't in the palace, yet his steward assured her that he had not left the city. Following the promptings of citizens who had seen him pass, Michal went out the gate of the city toward the north. There, beneath a rocky ledge just outside the city, she found the King of Israel, kneeling in prayer.

She stood in silence until David looked up. He rose quickly to his feet when he saw her and came to her, taking her hands in his. A great sorrow effused from his sapphire eyes. Michal noted how very blue and how very sad they were.

David stood, waiting for her to speak. He seemed to anticipate her question.

"Rizpah came to me," she told him. "She begged me to speak to you for her sons. She said that you will give them to the Gibeonites to be hanged."

Michal now waited for a response from David. His countenance changed, and he appeared confused.

"You have come to plead for Rizpah's children?" he asked, amazed.

"Why will you give them to the Gibeonites? Why will they be hanged?"

David frowned. "You have not heard," he stated. "You know that long ago Joshua made a league with the Amorites who lived in the city of Gibeon, thinking them to be from a far country?"

"Yes," Michal answered, somewhat impatiently.

"When King Saul sent to Nob and destroyed the city, many Gibeonites were killed as well as the families of the priests."

Michal said nothing, but the image swam before the eyes of her mind of the bloodied bodies of the priests that her father had massacred. She nodded.

David rubbed his eyes. "Israel got herself into this dilemma by making league with Gibeon instead of destroying her as the Lord had commanded." He sighed heavily and looked back into Michal's eyes. "The whole nation of Israel has suffered for three years because of what your father did to the Gibeonites."

Michal was confused.

"The famine," David said simply.

"How do you know this?" Michal asked defensively.

"The Lord told me," David said. Michal knew there could be no disputing him. The Lord did indeed speak to David.

"What has this to do with the sons of Rizpah?"

Great sadness spoke from the depths of David's soul through his eyes. A sob caught in his throat, which Michal could not fully grasp.

"I spoke to the elders of Gibeon and asked them what I could do for them to make an atonement so they would bless God's inheritance." Michal sensed that David spoke with great difficulty. "They didn't want silver or gold. They asked me to give them Saul's sons to be hanged in Gibeah." David's eyes pleaded for her understanding. "I had to give them. I have given my word to the Gibeonites."

"David, you know that the Scriptures say that children should not be put to death for their father's sin."[85]

David now wept. He sniffed and nodded. "That is what the Scriptures say. But it is neither God nor I who demands their death. It is the petition of Gibeon. It is the league with Gibeon which was breached."

"I hardly know them, but they are my brothers, David!" Michal hoped her personal plea might help to save Rizpah's sons.

David swallowed. Tears coursed down his face. He took both of her hands and fell before her on his knees.

"The Gibeonites asked for seven sons of Saul."[86]

Bewilderment pervaded her senses. Armoni and Mephibosheth, the sons of Rizpah, were the only living sons of Saul.

"Mephibosheth?" she whispered.

"No! My covenant with Jonathan protects him."

Slowly the obvious dawned upon Michal. Seven sons of Saul had been required.

---

[85] Deuteronomy 24:16

[86] II Samuel 21:8,9

"Who are the other five, David?" she demanded, beginning to tremble.

David's grief stooped his shoulders and he looked suddenly old and tired. "I had no choice, please believe me."

"No! Not my boys. You did not have to give them my boys!" she screamed. She fell to her knees, facing him squarely. "Please, David! Not my boys!"

David shook his head hopelessly. Michal did not hear David's answer. Blackness settled around her, and David caught her limp body as she crumpled.

CHAPTER 17

♦

THE PRINCESS ALONE

"Yea, though I walk through the valley of the shadow of death, I will fear no evil: for thou art with me; thy rod and thy staff they comfort me." Psalm 23:4

Michal awoke in a dim light. Jehoaddan sat beside her. As the memory revived she cried out. She bolted to her feet, and clutched her friend.

"My boys! I must see them!" She quieted instantly. "Do they still live?" she asked tremulously.

"Yes."

Michal learned that the seven sons of Saul were being held in the palace prison, to be delivered to the elders of the Gibeonites that very day. The guards let her pass, followed by Jehoaddan. Ignoring the fetid air and grime in the dim corridor, she hurried to the dungeon. It was a jug shaped pit in the ground, with the narrow neck opening wide enough only for a man to be squeezed through.

"I have come to see the sons of Merab, daughter of King Saul," she announced to the keeper of the dungeon.

"My Queen, they are in the hold and cannot be drawn up until they are delivered to the King." He paused. "King David," he added.

"Then lower me into the hold."

"Oh, my Queen, I can't do that!" The keeper began to tremble in fear.

Michal's grief allowed her no patience with the man. She glared at him testily. "Either bring them to me, or lower me into the hold," she commanded.

Reluctantly the keeper fitted a heavy rope around her, with lumps of rags beneath her arms for cushion. Jehoaddan stood by silently.

Michal did not feel the bite of the ropes against her flesh

as she was lowered into the dank hole. She was aware only of the torment in her heart.

When her feet hit the packed earth of the dungeon floor, she pulled the rope free. The only light filtered through the narrow neck of the dungeon, diffusing into the darkness around her. Before her eyes could grow accustomed to the darkness, she was suddenly embraced by strong arms.

"Aunt Michal!" a dear voice said, and a soft beard was brushed against her face.

"Joshua?" she asked into the darkness.

Other arms embraced her as her beloved boys greeted her. At last her eyes began to discern through the gloom, and she saw the bearded faces of Joel, Joshua, Jashub, and Adriel. As yet Saul was clean of face. She hugged them to her fiercely, fingering each face in the dimness, kissing each one in turn.

"Do you know why we were apprehended, Aunt Michal?" Joel asked gently.

"Yes," she answered through her tears.

"We have been told," said Joshua, "but we don't understand.

"Neither do I," she told them. "I spoke with David, but he believes he has no other choice."

"So we must die for our grandfather's sin?" asked Jashub.

Michal did not answer. Instead she mused, "Oh, if only I had Zerah, or Phaltiel! We would take you from David's men on the way to Gibeah and flee to freedom."

"We tried that once," Adriel reminded her, and a pain shot through her memory.

"It wouldn't matter," she said, drawing them close again. "You are on your way to..." She couldn't speak it.

Joshua grasped her shoulders firmly. "Aunt Michal," he said firmly. "Please don't go to Gibeah."

"We want you to remember us as we are now," Jashub said.

Joel touched her cheek and she faced him in the darkness.

"Will you look after my family? I have a wife and a son."

"I, too, have a wife. She is carrying my child. Will you look after them?" asked Joshua.

"Uncle Phaltiel's business belongs to them, now, and will be carried out by a trustworthy servant," Joel told her as she continued to weep. "But they will need more than financial support. If David will allow you, please assist them."

"I will, I promise I will. David will not keep me from it," Michal said.

"We will soon go to God," Joshua told her, and she wept anew. "We will see our mother, and Uncle Phaltiel. Don't sorrow for us."

"It is time," the keeper shouted down to them. He lowered the rope and Rizpah's sons appeared from the darkness and were hoisted up by turns. Michal was lifted next. Jehoaddan put her arm around her in support and comfort as her five boys were raised from the pit, one by one.

As their hands were bound, she pulled free from her friend and embraced each one again. Then she followed them along the dimly lit corridor and out into the courtyard. Suddenly blinded by the bright sunlight, she shaded her eyes and tried to see as her darlings were helped onto horses with lead reins, and, surrounded by armed soldiers, they were led out of the gate and away toward Gibeah.

Michal stood in the bright light staring at the empty gateway. Then her knees went limp and she fell back hard against her friend.

Michal was alone. Servants hovered near and Jehoaddan kept a watchful vigil, but she was alone. She could not let the thoughts form of her boys. They were gone. The grief laid against her heart as a great weight, constricting and suffocating. Darkness descended, and with it the sweet escape of sleep, allowing Michal to forget.

Her boys came to her in her dreams, smiling and laughing. They were young and free, as they had been when she had lived with them, when she and Phaltiel and her boys had been together. Michal awoke, disappointed that she had been dreaming. Then the remembrance came to her. Her boys were gone. She would neither eat nor speak. Jehoaddan came each day to stay with her. She held Michal's hand and spoke softly, often quoting the prayers of David. Michal could not be comforted. She hoped only that her physical body would soon succumb to her grief, so that she, too, may go to God.

Mephibosheth and Adah came. Mephibosheth knelt beside her, burying his face against her as he wept. "They died in my place," he repeated through his tears. "I loved them, Aunt Michal."

Michal opened her eyes and sighed. She lived still. She pulled herself up to sit against her pillows. Her emaciated limbs were weak and wasted. She did not wish to endure another day of life. Servants bathed and dressed her. Jehoaddan came and tried to coax sustenance between her lips. Michal turned her face away from her friend.

Suddenly David was kneeling at Michal's side. His copper curls were streaked with gray, and deep creases lined his handsome face. He bowed his head, and his shoulders shook. Michal watched him impassionately.

David lifted his face to her. His blue eyes were red with his tears. "Please forgive me, My Princess." He searched her eyes for understanding. "I never meant to cause you grief." David paused. His voice was hushed when he spoke. "I have been the cause of much grief to you, My Princess, yet I never desired to hurt you. Can you believe me? Can you forgive me? For the five sons of Merab? For the man Phaltiel?"

Michal looked into the dismal face of David. She had wept herself dry. She was weak from hunger. She did not wish to live. She was nothing in the kingdom of Israel. Yet, the great and powerful monarch of Israel bowed at her side. David, the shepherd king, begged her pardon. He had indeed caused her much sorrow. But as she looked into his eyes she knew that

David spoke the truth to her. She believed that he had meant no guile toward her, yet as the king, he had been duty bound to give her boys to Gibeon. There was no forgiving what he had done. But as Michal looked upon David, she held no malice toward him.

David straightened his shoulders. "My Princess, it is not good that you languish here in Jerusalem. I have learned that two of your nephews have wives and children. I think that it would be helpful to them," a pause, "and to you, if you were to go to Gallim. I have arranged a train to take you there."

David brought his face very close to hers. "Please, My Princess, go."

It would mean that her slow descent to death must cease. She would have to wait to go to God. David now asked her to go to the home in Gallim, the very place to which her heart had yearned through the years. Phaltiel was not there. Her boys were not there. But two young women who had loved her boys, and two small children who were part of her boys were there. She suddenly remembered the promise made in her last moments with her boys.

"Yes," she told David. "I will go."

Michal ate again, for she must regain her strength. Slowly, the vitality returned to arms and legs. She directed the packing of her belongings, making sure that she had the large scroll penned by the hand of Saul. "I will read to the children the stories from Scripture that their fathers loved," she told Jehoaddan. "They will learn to know their God." Anticipation brightened the days as she prepared to depart the palace of Jerusalem.

"Your Majesty," announced a servant at her door. She motioned him inside, and he entered, bearing a wooden chest bound with leather. "Shall I load this with your things?" he asked.

Michal ran her hand along the time smoothed wood and the rough leather. "Put it there," she told the man. Opening the latch, she found the black hooded robe. She pulled it from the confines and let the folds fall free. Tears coursed her face and tinged her voice as she handed it to the servant. "Burn this."

She fingered the shepherd's garb and sling. She lifted the small harp and plucked a string. Then replacing it, she closed the chest. She could not take the prayers of David with her.

"What shall I do with the chest, Your Majesty?" the man asked.

"Give it to the king," Michal told him. She turned and left the room forever.

214

EPILOGUE

King David is one of the best known and best loved kings of Israel's history, as well as the writer of most of the Psalms of the Scriptures. His life, as well as that of his first wife, Michal, are recorded in the books of I and II Samuel. David knew from his youth that God had chosen him to be the King of Israel. However, being a very human man, David was not perfect, and he caused himself much grief and many family problems because of his disobedience to God's command that a king should not multiply wives.

Throughout his life, David loved and sought after the Lord God. God says of him, "I have found David the son of Jesse, a man after mine own heart, which shall fulfill all my will." Acts. 13:22. The Lord Jesus Christ, God the Son who was born in the flesh, came through the family line of David. Jesus Christ shed His blood and died to pay the penalty for our sins. He then arose from the dead to give us eternal life if we will believe Him and receive the gift. "For God so loved the world that He gave His only begotten Son, that whosoever believeth in Him should not perish, but have everlasting life." John 3:16